2359 HOURS

2359 HOURS

Jack B.S. North

To the traumatized.

AUTHOR PRESENCE

ADDITIONAL TITLES BY JACK B.S. NORTH

Simon's Death

Early Exit To The Void

ONLINE PRESENCE

Twitter @JackBSNorth

jacknorth.ca

AUTHOR'S NOTE

THEY SAY CHARACTERS spring out of an author's imagination, but a few years ago, the character showed up one day and demanded I tell his story. Archie occupied my mind powerfully while I whipped off the first draft. But it's taken me awhile to finish his story because...

TRIGGER WARNING FOR NOVEL

Archie's story was difficult to write, and it's difficult to read with all the trauma coursing through him. Having someone on standby, or a dog or cat to hold, while you immerse yourself in his day of remembering, may help.

His story will stay with me for my lifetime. I'm glad he showed up and told me to tell it.

THANK YOUS

Because of the context of this novel, I want to thank anonymously the generous people who helped me.

The gun store owner who viewed me suspiciously and interrogated me until satisfied I was genuinely there to learn about guns. I may not be a fan—bit of an understatement there—but as a writer, you have to learn about what your character feels comfortable with, likes to use, and wants in their life. Research is research is research. It's not up to me to judge and say, "No, I'm not seeing it from his point of view." Or "I don't wanna learn!" Also, I think gotcha journalism or writing is inherently dishonest. Good research begins with honesty with the people you're interviewing or learning from.

I want to thank the US Army veteran who overcame his own pain to answer my multitude of questions, and his mother who introduced us. I want to thank my long-standing friend for sending me many links to help my understanding along. I thank the psychiatrist who evaluated my depiction of PTSD and warned me it was so on point, it would trigger people. Hence, the trigger warning!

I want to thank NaNoWriMo for creating a space to let one's imagination fly and Prolifiko for providing the structure and impetus to finish this story. And EG for their feedback, from detailed to overarching points, and their reactions to Archie and his story. They all made this novel possible!

PROLOGUE

"WHAT DO YOU see, Archie?"

"Sky?" Archie asked his grandfather hesitantly.

"Is that all?" Pawpaw replied.

Archie craned his neck to search Pawpaw's face for clues. They were sitting on the hood of Pawpaw's blue and white battered pickup truck; Archie concentrated hard on the question while trying to ignore the metal searing his bottom through his jeans, its scorched smell combining with the arid air. The engine ticked quietly as it recovered from the long drive under the blasting sun. The sun's rays beat heat down on their heads under the wide sky. Pawpaw squinted into the distance, lines etched into his leathery skin on either side of his eyes.

Archie scrunched his face to copy his grandfather's. *Maybe I can see what Pawpaw sees if I squint,* Archie thought.

He scanned the distance. "Brown?"

Pawpaw choked back a sound. Archie sided his eyes. *Is Pawpaw mad like Sir always is? Pawpaw's lips are wriggling funny.*

Pawpaw glanced down at Archie's fair hair, shorn down to fingernail-width length. It looked like he was readying to join the military. Pawpaw hoped not. He'd like Archie to ranch like he did, ride the wild grassland and see the rough country as a land of opportunity, not stay shut up in the city of Albuquerque.

"Look again, son." He pointed a gnarled finger.

Archie followed Pawpaw's tanned finger, its skin grooved in lines that lead to his yellowed fingernail, the end joint swollen and bending down to the ground. Archie looked past the familiar finger and tried squeezing his cheeks up to his eyes. He said, "Sand."

"What else?" Pawpaw asked again, his voice slow with patience with his six-year-old grandson.

"Bushes."

"What kind of bushes did I tell you they were?"

"Sagebrush."

"That's right."

Archie smiled as he ducked his head and noticed the scatter of white coffee cups under his dangling feet. "Why are there so many cups, Pawpaw?"

Pawpaw grunted, "It's urbanites with no use for nature. Don't you become one, Archie."

"I won't, Pawpaw! I promise!"

"Good boy. It isn't only the Indians who respect land. It can't give you anything if you don't treat it nice. Remember that."

"I'll remember!"

"You be like the desert, Archie. Vast, hidden, open."

Archie moved his lips, mouthing, "Vast. Hidden. Open."

"Don't be like your father and look down on other people. We all have a right to live."

Archie swallowed. He swung his feet back and forth, like opposing metronomes, thinking how he was supposed to respect Sir, his father. But Pawpaw said to ignore him, like he always did on these long drives out of Albuquerque to the desert or forest. Sagebrush. Desert. Forest. Archie focused on those words. He liked the desert best of all. It let him see forever, and it was so quiet. Only his grandfather and the ticking of the cooling engine spoke.

Sometimes the wind sighed past them. Here, he was safe with Pawpaw, learning to be like him. Archie stopped swinging his feet on that thought. He lifted his head and smiled up into his grandfather's watchful face. "I'll remember. We all have a right to live. I'll remember that, Pawpaw."

Pawpaw smiled.

0001 HOURS

Chapter

1

TODAY.

THE THOUGHT strikes Archie like a grandfather clock's bong.

Dim white light scratches his peripheral vision, demanding his attention.

Archie jerks his head around.

His heart flips, flops, tumbles around in his chest, winding up his mind into a screech.

12:01.

One minute past midnight. Not 0001 as it should be, but 12:01. Civilian time. Archie hates this digital clock ticking time down as if it's another ordinary day. He craves Pawpaw's analogue clock: only Pawpaw's grassland-experienced, war-weary, faithful clock is allowed to show time in twelve hours in Archie's mind. But Pawpaw's clock is broken.

The digital clock's dim numbers flare their shapes into his retina. Archie shuts his eyelids tight and can see the numbers in the blackness behind like he has night vision. With a gasp, his eyelids pop open. The silent numbers greet him, unchanged.

Time is broken.

It remains one minute after midnight.

Archie stretches his ears out into the first minute of the new day. It heralds silently the deepening night.

Like Pawpaw's travel alarm clock, absence is a sound.

His grandfather's old wind-up travel alarm clock with its fading white face and steel arms and numerals, in its worn tan leather case had decided to stop ticking time yesterday. Archie had snuggled it into his jacket pocket yesterday morning—as he'd set out on his walk of the city. For once, he'd had a goal: find a clock repair shop. He had. Within an hour, he'd spotted a glass window filled with old clocks from grandfathers to steely alarm clocks. He'd entered time's sanctum with its gold flat carpeting and its glass case straddling the back wall across from the glass door with its diagonal handle. A man about his age responded to the tiny bell's tinkling as Archie had entered and had arrived on his side of the case as Archie had from the door side.

"Can I help you?"

Archie had fished out the travel clock, opened it, and placed it with its face facing the man. "Can you repair this?"

The man had picked it up, studied it, then looked up at Archie. "My grandfather can, but he's not here. He's gone to Florida and'll be back in April. Can you wait until then?" He'd handed the clock back to Archie. Archie had taken it, snuggled it into his jacket pocket, nodded once, turned on his heel, and left. He'd had no choice but to buy a new clock, with its 12-hour numbers, to replace Pawpaw's.

Archie lets his head fall back into its natural position of face up to the ceiling. He squeezes his eyes shut, hoping for sleep to return so that he can stop thinking about clocks and time. The seconds tick on in his mind. Psychic pain floods his chest. Then suddenly...nothing.

Detachment separates Archie from his frustration. He'd left the frozen-in-time shop and had stopped outside its door. He'd inhaled deeply as he'd steeled himself to turn his booted feet towards the bustling and always-being-renovated Eaton Centre, which contained a familiar Best Buy. Dread had filled Archie as he'd joined the cacophonous mass of people swirling in through the Eaton Centre's revolving glass doors, around its balconies and indoor trees, into its snaking halls, threading themselves chaotically into the shops. The noise of many voices and endless feet had pummelled his head. People had zig-zagged into Archie, bent on their missions, unheeding of the paths of others. Panic had screamed into his heart and flailed at his ribs. Archie had lunged into Best Buy, careened towards the aisle with clocks, and snatched up the first one he'd seen. He'd hustled to the cashier area, only to have to wait in line. His nerves had stretched and stretched till thin strands of packed-in electrons tensed his muscles, causing his feet to stir as his mind fought his body's desire to run.

As his fingers had begun to let go of his intended purchase so that he could flee, unhindered, the cashier had called out, "Next!" Tension had blown out as he hustled to her counter, paid for his clock, and speed-walked out the automatic sliding glass doors. Relief had sagged his straight back as he'd walked far from Bay and Dundas, away from the shopping crowds who were bent on the hunt for pleasure through spending.

Reminding himself he's flat on his back in his bed, Archie exhales the memory hard.

He has yet to figure out how to change his clock to the 24-hour time.

Archie grimaces and closes his eyes against the dim, screeching numbers, now showing 12:02.

Squealing brakes fling his eyes open. A woman swears at the driver: "Watch where you're fucking going, you fucking moron!

Don't you know this is a fucking residential street, you fucking turd?"

Apparently not, Archie thinks. *And neither does she,* he adds morosely. *Most drivers don't. Not Toronto drivers.* Archie had heard that the politicians had reduced the speed limit, but he'd seen no evidence of it.

Archie hates Toronto drivers. All drivers.

He has no use for them or desire to be one of them.

He walks to where he wants to go.

I should sleep, he grouses, his consciousness returning to his present dusky surroundings, as the car screams down the street away from his closed single-pane window with its old, crooked blinds that let in the streetlight in ribs of light and shadows on his walls.

Rapid clicking of a woman's heels follows the car into the night.

Silence returns to the street.

Archie lowers his eyelids. He turns his mind to the muscles in his forehead. He tenses them as he begins his relaxation exercise, the one his last VA counsellor had taught him, the only man the VA had assigned to his care who'd understood his mood, his pain, his isolation. The only man who'd buoyed him up; the only person he had looked forward to seeing all week.

And then the VA had taken him away.

And now here he, Archie, lies in Toronto, in a rooming house on a dark November night far away from the searing sun of his home and the wretched dirt of Afghanistan, unable to sleep. *The Canadians I flew here to join are probably in their own beds wide awake, too,* Archie thinks. It brings him no comfort.

Today.

Archie releases his lips into a sigh of grief as he lets the word into his consciousness. He blinks until his eyes dry out. But his chest refuses to give up its cache of sobs. What does a broken heart look like on an ECG? "All normal," the VA cardiologist had declared, before slapping his file shut and ushering him out the door. How can his heart be normal when every day an elephant sits on it and the pain devil squeezes it on either side until he's gasping for air? The scans and EEGs, the VA neurologist had lectured him, are all normal. "Get on with your life, and you'll be fine," he'd declared. Only his counsellor had listened to him until he'd run out of words. His brows curl up as he remembers how his body had released its burden for one moment that first day in the man's office. He'd begun to speak a few words, a couple words at a time, his consciousness on high alert, scanning the face and body language of this new man supposedly provided to cure him. The new VA counsellor had frowned in thought and empathy at Archie's sparse words. Archie had doubted the veracity of this persona he presented. *Could he really be hearing him?* The counsellor had furrowed his brow into the silence Archie had let fall. He'd leaned forward, clasping his rough tanned hands. Then he'd looked up into Archie's eyes, his brown ones softening, and had said: "You are broken. But you can be healed. I will teach you. I will help you. And I will never give up on you." Archie had heard the words but hadn't felt them. The counsellor had said, "It's okay, Archie. I will show you I'm here for you." Over the weeks, by degrees, Archie had begun to believe that here was one man who heard him, one person who wouldn't give up on him.

The roughness of the sheet under his curling right hand returns Archie to the present. He blinks at the yellowed white of the ceiling with its splotches of smoky stains, its little flakes that point toward the floor like tiny signposts, its meandering crack that in his almost two years of staring at it has crept from one corner of the room towards the middle. It hasn't reached the middle yet with its lone, feeble bare LED bulb—Archie had replaced the incandescent with the LED light when he'd moved in—and he wonders when it will. He wonders if he will see it reach that round white-metal base of the light fixture.

Today.

Archie flings away the thought that word brings and focuses on musing where the glass shade for the fixture had gone. He stares at the large bulbous shape of the LED so that its solidity will replace the images lodged deep in his brain. The LED seems to grow and fill his sight. Another car gunning down the street shatters his exercise of blanking his mind.

Archie's in Afghanistan, his commanding officer yelling, "Gun it! Faster!" as he's driving down a dusty, pit-holed road, all his hip and leg and foot muscles pushing the accelerator of the convoy truck down hard as he steers with all his fingers and thumbs wrapped around the steering wheel to keep it from jouncing out of his control. The smells of the heat, the sweat pouring from underneath the armpits of his superior sitting next to him, the dust clouding up around the spinning wheels of his truck, assail his nostrils. The roar of the engine as he accelerates drowns his ears. The sight of endless desert brown through the dust caking his windshield assaults his vision. His heart thuds hard against his ribs; he pants. The voice of his VA counsellor penetrates Archie's internal repeating movie: "Inhale deeply. Tell yourself the year and place you're in. Replace the memory with the present. Do it!"

Archie inhales deeply, hoping to replace the memory with the actual smells of his room. "Ground yourself," Archie hears his VA counsellor's voice call out from the distance of time. He strains to inhale clean smells of lemon, bleach, and pine. Archie mops the floor every day with lemon floor oil, he cleans the walls with bleach, he scrubs the floor near the door with pine cleaner, anything to replace the smells of dirt and fear with the peaceful, clean smells of city life in a country that's the closest to home he'll have on this earth. But he still smells fear. Archie tells himself the date: Remembrance Day. November 11th. He yells out: "Toronto!"

Suddenly, Archie is back in his room. The silence deafens him. A sob from his own mouth interrupts it. Archie clamps his hand over his teeth to stifle it. He's so sick of crying. He's sick of the memories.

And that wasn't even the worst one. Pain lances his soul. He sucks his lips in between his teeth and bites hard. Physical pain spreads into Archie's wet cheeks as memory stabs his consciousness and his hand slips down to his sheets.

The VA had taken from him the one counsellor who'd promised to stick with him. Archie had shown up one day at his weekly appointment and been told that they'd transferred his counsellor to another VA hospital, and they'd assign him a new guy. *Not again!* Archie had flamed to himself. He didn't want another new guy. The third counsellor they'd assigned him had been it. Archie's chest had burned with his need to see his patient, caring, listening counsellor. He'd clamped his lips tight. With a squeak of heel on mopped floor, he'd turned and walked out. He'd walked home, packed, walked out of the family home, and flown to Canada with his insanity, his health, his desire to…

In Canada's biggest city, Archie had hoped to heal with his Canadian army buddies, the ones who'd welcomed him into their unit in that dusty country. But healing is a long, winding road with no end in sight, a road pockmarked with pain, with crevasses so cavernous you can't see them until you've fallen in and find yourself even more alone than you had been before. Every time, his Canadian army buddies had pulled him out. How many times can they do that? How many times will he want to?

Weariness drags every fibre of Archie's muscles down until he feels like a lead plug.

I can't go on.

The knowledge sinks into Archie.

Indelible images appear of the dead, limbs shredded from their torsos, hands blackened lying on their own far away from their arms, feet blasted apart. Archie's heart raises its beating tempo to one hundred, one hundred and twenty, one hundred and fifty. Sweat pops out on Archie's forehead. Archie sees the men alive, with him in their tight quarters, telling stories, guffawing and slapping their thighs as they swigged beer together in their sweaty tans. His lips quirk upwards in remembered happiness. Then their gruesome bodies insert themselves again into his vision. Archie's pulse shoots up to one hundred and eighty. Faint words from the listening counsellor speak through the metronome of death: "Ground yourself."

Archie reaches out his left hand to the object glinting in the light of the alarm clock's numbers. With his fine, long fingers, he touches its hard handle, he traces the in-and-out contours above the handle, he strokes the long, cold metal. Archie retracts his hand back to his side, to lay it on the bed beside his leg underneath the white sheet and white sleeping bag as his heart slows down and drops below a hundred. His forehead dries.

Today, I will escape, Archie assures himself. *I will end this eternal pain. My story is over.*

Comfort and relief flow out of Archie's head and into his body, relaxing him into the thin foam of a mattress many have lain on before him, burying him into the rough sheet that covers the foam that he's lying on.

Archie sleeps.

A dream startles his eyes open. The dream vanishes, the words remain: *I still have a story to tell.*

<u>0122 HOURS</u>

Chapter
2

MEMORY SQUEEZES ITS arms around Archie's body, deceives his mind that the past is the present. Archie's heart revs up.

Archie shoots straight into the air, flinging the top sheet and sleeping bag halfway down his bed, and lands on his feet next to his bed. He hunches down and darts his head around to scrutinize the blinds covering the window; the middle slat with its metal bent one-third of the way along its length seems to wiggle. He drops his head while keeping his eyes straight forward. Archie sniffs the air. It's a blend of the pine floor cleaner he uses and musty wood. Yet the familiar odours don't allay him. Archie bends his knees so that his legs are ready to spring if needed and simultaneously bends his elbows and keeps his arms at waist height in case they need to strike.

Archie creeps toward the blinded window, one soft footstep at a time, like a tiger stalking its prey. He reaches them in three steps. His eyes do not blink. The bent slat doesn't move. His corneas dry. The blinds remain still. Archie's muscles ache from the strain of immobility, of vigilance, of remaining ready to leap forward or crouch down. But the blinds, including their bent slat, don't move. The minutes tick past in Archie's mind.

Slowly, rational thought tickles the edges of Archie's brain: the slat is not a threat.

Archie uncoils himself, straightens his arms, straightens his legs, and lifts his head. He shakes his head and shoulders, letting his arms sway unguarded with his movement, letting the tension leave his body. He reaches his right hand up, and his fingers arrow in between the bent slat and the one above. Using his fingers to spread the two slats apart, Archie peers through the gap. The quiet street greets his sight. The old metal-halide-white streetlights light up the grey sidewalks in their hostile artificiality. Ribbons of tar gleam in the lights' glare along the asphalt road. Ragged trees reaching crooked branches to the lit-up sky, clinging to their few leaves, provide pockets of darkness on either side of the road. Archie stretches out his ears and listens. In the distance, traffic creates steady white noise, but no cars turn on to his street. Archie releases the slats, and they clash back into place. The blinds bang against the window in a fading rhythm.

Archie turns around and pads back to his bed. He drops onto his bed and wriggles his feet underneath the top sheet. The night air has cooled it. He pulls up to his armpits the chilled top white sheet and the white sleeping bag Andrew had given him. A Canadian army one for the Arctic. His body is used to desert heat not clammy Toronto November cold; the Arctic sleeping bag warms him. The whiteness of his bedding soothes him. Archie's body re-warms the crumpled sheet underneath him. He stretches his long legs under the gathering warmth, bends his elbows, and laces his fingers behind the back of his head. His eyes cannot close. Archie turns his head to check his clock: 1:22. He doesn't react; instead, he turns his head back to contemplate the ceiling.

Archie's mind blanks out. All he sees, all he knows, is that ceiling above him, staring back down at him, the flakes growing larger in his vision, the crack meandering off the flat two-dimensional surface and reaching an accusing end down toward him. Archie watches it draw closer to him with no reaction, no emotion, no thought.

Archie blinks.

And the crack is just a crack on the ceiling. The flakes are tiny bits of old paint losing their adherence.

Archie yawns.

Briefly, a wish to be asleep and not awake, to be able to put his head down and sleep eight hours straight like he used to, enters Archie's thoughts. Archie brushes them away as he pulls his right hand out from behind his head to wipe his eyes. He puts his hand back behind his head to cradle it with its left companion. The air stills itself into infinite silence. In his internal ears, he can hear Pawpaws's travelling clock tick each second off. It had witnessed many mornings of battle. This new clock is soundless. It's all visual. It's seen nothing and so is not broken.

Like the endless road before him as he drove one of the convoy trucks month after month on one of his tours in Afghanistan.

Archie blinks.

Archie doesn't want to remember the desert or the truck or the men riding with him being blown to bits or his superior losing his leg or the VA tossing him out like so much junk, as if one counsellor is the same as the next. Archie particularly doesn't want to remember...

Archie shakes his head. Left, right, left, right, one cheek then the other one slamming into his pillow, his mouth opening in a silent scream, tears sliding out of his eyes and dripping toward his ears. His hands leave off cradling his head and grip the short, spiked thick hair on the back of his skull and his elbows pull together to hide his face. Archie shuts his eyes. His legs bend and straighten in a parody of running.

No.

No memory.

It's over.

It's done with.

They made their decision. And I made mine, he reminds himself.

I'm safe here in Canada, away from abandonment, away from rejection, away from the people who loved me the most.

Or so they'd said.

Archie stops. He opens his eyes. His eyes look to the wall on his right; his right leg is bent while his left is straight. He mouths the date: *November eleventh.* He tells himself where he is: *Toronto.* He straightens his right leg as his hands release his hair. Slowly, slowly, his shoulders loosen and his arms drop to his side.

"I'm not like the desert anymore, Pawpaw," Archie whispers. He draws up into his nose the scents of his room to remind his brain where he is. A rainy city.

Archie begins his relaxation exercise. He tenses his forehead and prays for sleep.

He'd forgotten to pray last night, Archie realizes with a start. Better do it now.

Archie begins to recite out loud to the uncaring room: "Our Father..." Archie stops. *I can't pray*, he moans silently to himself. Who is listening? Who cares? Does anyone? Not the ones who loved him the most, so why would God? Emotional pain feeds into each neuron, and the surface of his body aches and burns. Where is God? God had been a vague figure back home. Only when he'd arrived in Afghanistan, facing the hostile landscape and hostile forces within and without, had he begun to ask this question. One of the men, as he was being shipped home, had suggested to Archie he go to the prayer meetings the chaplain held regularly, whenever he could. Archie had sat on the outskirts of the circle, listened to the stories, and felt the prayers flowing peace into him. That one oasis of peace became a necessity in the middle of the hatred and fear layering violence upon violence all around him.

Archie arches his neck in a futile attempt to stare straight through the ceiling above him, through the room above him, through the roof above him, to see the heavens and God. But all Archie sees is the faint lightness of the yellowed-white paint above. He searches for God, and God remains hidden on the other side of the barrier that his childhood had begun to build and Afghanistan had finished.

Archie sighs and straightens his head. He consciously relaxes his body until both legs and both arms slightly angle away from it. Eyelids closing, he begins his relaxation exercise again. He stalls at the frowning start. *Why?*

There is no answer. And he's not one for futile questions; yet there it is, hanging in the space of his brain that's lit with pain: the question behind his story.

Archie draws his brows together harder and squeezes his eyes shut so tight, points of light pop into his view. Archie forcibly releases the tension then moves on to tensing his cheeks and letting them drop back slack before tightening his jaw and compressing his lips. He arches his neck until the stretch pains the front and the pull his upper back. Archie straightens his neck with relief, then hunches his shoulders up to his ears, leaves them there for fifteen long seconds, and lets them go. With each contraction and each letting go, he relaxes and drifts towards sleep.

A FOOTFALL. Outside his door. Archie snaps out of bed, grabs his Smith & Wesson, and is standing beside his door with its five locks and new steel hinges protected by two thick steel plates screwed into the door frame underneath the moulding on either side of the door.

Archie waits. He slows his breathing down until he is a shadow amongst the other unmoving shadows in his room. Archie attunes his nose to the sickly sweetness wafting through the cracks he cannot fill. Alcohol.

"I know you're in there!" The bellow erupts from the other side of the door. Archie doesn't twitch.

"You can't hide from me, you nasty little American. Yeah, I know you're illegal here. I ought to report ya!" A crash punctuates this remark as the man charges his door. Archie recognizes the fuming voice: Nadine's ex. The rooming house seems to hold its breath. Archie asks himself while keeping his focus on the man and his door: *How did he find me?*

Only his Canadian unit knows he lives here. Archie has kept under the radar. He hasn't allowed himself to get sick or seek government assistance for anything. Archie's still an American where your country takes care of its soldiers but you take care of yourself.

A body smacking against the door, a groan cut short, draws his focus back to the threat.

"I know you're in there! You wife-stealing bastard!"

No point in arguing with an angry drunk. Arguments like that degenerate into a schoolyard rally of taunts. Waste of breath. The best offence is a defence. But Archie doesn't relax, doesn't assume the door will hold. This man is determined. Archie debates whether to open it and take him out. Archie considers the long barrel of his gun. If it goes off, its thunderous bang reverberating off the hard surfaces of this closed room will bring the cops and then the government and then the legal system. Archie grimaces in disgust. He walks over to his bed and slips the weapon underneath the flimsy mattress. Archie walks back to his vigil. Meanwhile, Nadine's ex continues to bludgeon the door and is no longer cutting off his groans as the wood bruises his flesh and the steel holds the door firm against his assault.

Archie stands ready. Nadine's ex is weakening on the other side of the door. Archie hears Rufus slam open his room door down at the end of the hall. The acrid scent of his unwashed body reaches his memory, and Archie's nostrils involuntarily close. Archie sees the unfolding drama before it happens—Rufus thin from heroin use, muscles emaciated, mind haunted by the sight of a boy being raped in Afghanistan and being unable to move to help, unlike the rest of his unit who had rescued the boy and had given a lesson to the man he hadn't forgotten. Rufus's mind had chosen to disappear rather than act to his everlasting shame. Now any time he hears another being threatened, Rufus storms out on his tottery stick legs to help and inevitably ends up in the hospital.

Archie can't allow that.

Archie swiftly, soundlessly, unlocks each well-oiled lock. He whips open his door; Nadine's ex stumbles in; Archie grabs his arm as the ex trips by; whips him around; and marches him out his door and down the hall to the stairs, while calling out sotto voce to Rufus: "I got it." Rufus can hear a pin drop on the other side of the house and three floors down. Over the swearing from the man in his hold, Archie waits to hear Rufus go back into his room and close the door. Then he says to Nadine's ex: "You have two choices. You continue as you are, and I let go, and you fall down the stairs. Or you walk down them and out the door and never come back of your own accord."

"I know what you and Nadine are doing, you American filth." Nadine's ex twists his head and exhales into Archie's face, and Archie wants to vomit. Instead, he snuffles up the sour smell and blows out through his mouth, attempting to habituate to the revolting odour while calming himself.

"You're mad at her. You're mad at yourself for losing a fine woman. I get it," Archie says.

"You took her from me—,"

"I know it feels like that," Archie replies in an even tone, while resisting the ex's attempts to escape his hold. "But if you think about it, it's not true, is it?"

"It is!" Nadine's ex gasps as he exerts sudden energy and it rebounds along his muscle fibres against the immovable rock wall of Archie.

"Really?"

"You would say that, wouldn't you? You're the one she's having an affair with!" Pain flares up the man's anger again.

Archie shifts forwards until the drunken man's toes extend over the edge of the landing. Nadine's ex rears back but cannot reverse from his precarious place on the staircase's top edge against Archie's solidity. The ex clamps his teeth together with an audible click. "I'm right," he grits out.

"Are you?" Archie asks. "Or are you looking for a way out from your pain?" Archie angles forward, forcing the ex's head to lean over the stairs, forcing him to look down at the bare wooden steps, their edges blackened and their middles sagging from a century of use. The ex fights for breath.

"She left me," he half-moans, half-yells.

"She did. I don't enjoy being dumped either." Archie snaps his mouth shut and stays in place, letting his body speak its implacable message that Archie is the stronger. The rooming house's hushed fear, the stench of people not wanting to get involved, surrounds Nadine's ex and Archie as Archie pinions him until the ex realizes that the only way out is down on his own two feet. Nadine's ex huffs, one, two, three times, until all breath escapes him like a deflating balloon. "Alright, I'll go."

Archie barely stabilizes him, lets him go, and steps back out of his reach. The ex's left foot slides off the landing and onto the top step; he lurches as his right foot follows; he grabs the balustrade to prevent himself tumbling down. His forward momentum takes him down like a drunken sailor several more steps, while Archie watches, until he can catch his balance and slow his chaotic descent. Nadine's ex half jogs down a few steps. He angles his head to the left to look out the far corner of his eye up at Archie, standing above him in the twilight hallway. He steps down, one, two, three stairs before twisting around fully to growl up at him: "This ain't over." Nadine's ex leaps over the bottom three steps down to the first floor landing and struts out of sight toward the front door. Archie listens for the door opening and slamming shut. He listens for breathing, for footsteps. Nothing. Nadine's ex has left.

Soft footfalls make his ears twitch. *Was I wrong? Is that drunk back?* Archie narrows his eyes downwards as his body vibrates with attention toward the sound. Rufus's grey-and-white cat pads rapidly up the steps into his view. She skirts around him, trotting towards Rufus's door. Suddenly, he recalls his VA counsellor's words: that when he becomes vigilant, when he reaches for his gun, then he's to remember things are less likely threats than just another sound or action in daily life. Civilian life in America is not military life in Afghanistan. Even less is Canadian civilian life, where people don't routinely carry. Archie hears his counsellor's words replaying in his head: "Reaching for your gun is the first sign you're not in control." Archie flushes with shame that he'd forgotten advice he used to remember when seeing the counsellor. The man had explained: "When you reach for your gun, what's in control are the memories associated with loud shouts from men, with bangs and thuds, and those memories trigger your sensitized stress response system. They are in control."

Archie groans. He is to ground himself first. He's to breathe deeply, rhythmically, to put his thinking self back in control.

Back in the present, standing in the rooming house's hallway, as still as a weathered statue, he watches the cat trotting towards Rufus. Not a threat, but he'd reacted as if she was.

Archie returns wearily to his room and its open door while keeping his ears cocked for human sounds or movements of air behind him. He can't help himself. A soft meow wafts down the hall towards him. He pauses and trains his ears towards the sound. The last door on the same side of the hall opens; she zips in with a huffy yowl. The door clicks closed. A lock tumbles into place. The house creaks; groans ooze faintly out from behind a couple of doors down the hallway. Archie walks through his door and shuts it behind himself. He leans against it for seconds before turning around and locking all five locks methodically. The clean scents of the floor oil and cleaner from his nightly mopping reassures him.

Archie walks to his bed and bends down towards his mattress to fish out his grandfather's weapon. Archie lays it back ready and on guard on the nightstand. He flops down onto his bed and covers himself up with his white sheet and white sleeping bag and stares sightlessly up at the ceiling. He is so wide awake he despairs he will ever sleep again.

Sleep comes.

Memory becomes the present.

As Archie dreams of the dead he left behind.

0223 HOURS

Chapter 3

"TELL ME," SAYS Archie's VA counsellor as he leans forward, elbows on his thighs, hands between his knees.

It's a dream, a voice somewhere in the distance, says into the deceiving reality gripping Archie. The repeating dream-distorted memory obliterates the voice, and he's immersed in the past, in the dream, believing the past is happening now.

Archie slides his hands down his face and slopes down into his chair. His heart lurches into his stomach. He closes his eyes and searches for the courage. "I...," But he can't tell his counsellor what happened. Sally is there before his eyes, her face taunting him as she upbraids him: "What's wrong with you? We need the money, and you're spending it on beer with your buddies!" Sally's clutched hand with its stretched-out forefinger grows large in his eyes until her finger's point pierces his forehead and slides through his brain like an arrow through whipped cream. Archie gasps for air. "What's the matter with you? Can't you take a little criticism. Baby." That's Sir, his father, speaking. Archie swivels his head to look at his father's scowling face, the lines in his forehead like furrows in rich red PEI soil ready for planting.

Potatoes, Archie thinks. Suddenly, fries cut in thin strips frying in hot oil assails his nostrils. Acrid smoke from burning oil as the base's truck burns in the burn pit flies into his face along with the sand that the wind whips up from the desert.

"Tell me about it," intones his counsellor, his solemnity like church bells calling parishioners from the killing fields to confess their sins to their God.

Archie sweats blood. Sickly, salty red drips into his eyes, shading all that he sees the colour of death. Blood is everywhere. It's spattered all over him.

"Why did you do that?" Sally yells accusingly.

"*Do what?*"

"Spend our food money on your booze."

"I don't drink," he says, confused.

"That's the problem with you," Sir accuses him from behind his head. "You're not a real soldier. Real soldiers aren't health nuts," he spits contempt, and honey hits the floor in sticky drops. Archie watches honey ooze towards his naked feet, morphing from blonde to rust to bright crimson, pulsing with dying life as it touches his toes, crawls onto his feet, burns its way up his ankles, his shins, his thighs. The metamorphosing goo screams: "You're not a real soldier. You're not a man. You're useless."

"Tell me about it," his counsellor asks kindly. Archie swivels his head back around, all the way around to face forward. His counsellor's head explodes. Brain and guts and slices of skin spatter him like grease spitting from a smoking pan.

Archie sits up screaming, ejecting the dream and throwing himself back into the present, the mundane present of his nightly changing-the-sheets ritual and the wall behind his head pounding like a rhythmic nail gun. "Shut up!" the wall screams in concert with Archie's vocal cords. Sweat spews out of Archie's scalp, soaking his hair. Sweat cascades down his face and drips off his chin to join the flood wetting his skin and stinking up his sheets.

Archie stops screaming.

"Every fucking night!" the wall shouts. "I'm gonna talk to the landlord about you. He's gonna kick you out, and I'm gonna get my sleep." A last bang on the wall punctuates his threat.

Archie pants into the resounding silence. Sleep. He shuts his eyes, desperate for dreamless sleep. Nightmare-less sleep. Dry sleep.

Archie opens his eyes and lifts his head. His sopping wet sheets and boxer briefs greet his sight. Archie swings his legs out from underneath the cooling top sheet and plants his feet on the old wooden boards of his floor, wrinkling his nose at the pungency steaming from his body. He must attend to his ritual. He must slow his heartbeat, as his VA counsellor, the one who'd helped him, had advised.

"Ritual, Archie," his counsellor had said, leaning forward and capturing Archie's darting eyes with his own steady ones. "Ritual, Archie, is the key to a steady rhythm of your heart and your life."

Archie pushes himself up by his fists and stands there, swaying from tiredness, his head drooping. *Where is my sleeping bag?* Archie sucks in a lungful of air and lifts his head. Shoving out all thoughts, he turns around to strip off his sheets and pull the beaten-up pillow out of its case. He lobs them into the hamper sitting beside the distressed dresser. After a moment, he pads to his dresser, strips off his briefs, and tosses them into the hamper on top of the bedding. He pulls out a fresh pair of grey boxer briefs from the dozen filling the top drawer and pulls them on. He glides over to the cedar chest at the bottom of the bed. The chest is his one indulgence. As he reaches it, he spots his sleeping bag on the floor on the other side of the bed. Ignoring the bag for the moment, he raises the lid of the chest and, holding on to the lid with his left hand, with his right hand he lifts out a bundle of two sheets and a pillowcase from the pile of bundles of sheets and pillowcases sorted and ready to make the bed. He carries the bundle of sheets and pillowcase to the nightstand and drops them there. The bundle covers the nightstand's metal possession. Archie swiftly takes hold of the bottom sheet to remove it from the bundle and snaps the sheet over the mattress, yanking it straight. Archie tucks the sheet under each corner with hospital corners. Grasping the top sheet, he whips it loose of its folds and lets it float onto the bed. He tucks in the two bottom corners, turns down the top of the sheet, turns the pillowcase inside out, slides his hands in to the corners of it, grasps two corners of the pillow through the pillowcase, and expertly pulls the pillow into its case. He drops the freshly encased pillow onto the head of the bed, walks round to the side of the bed opposite the window to pick up his sleeping bag, and whisks it over the top sheet. Archie's heart settles down; his breathing slows; his shoulders drop; and his hands uncurl. The ritual has done its work. Its boring sameness had protected him from the chaotic entwining of his memories and dreams.

Archie walks back to the window side of the bed and stares down at his gun lying on his nightstand.

His grandfather's gun. Pawpaw's companion.

Bits of brain fling themselves into his eyes; blood spatters his nose, his cheeks, his chin; and the distant roar of gunfire, punctuated by exploding IEDs, rushes toward him from the street outside. Archie vacuums air deep into his lungs. He's here in Toronto. Not America. Not Afghanistan. Canada. Peaceful Canada.

The gun is by itself again, its coating of brain and blood gone.

Archie stares at it, reaches out a tentative hand, snatches it back, and collapses on his bed, his head falling between his knees. Tears slip down his face and plop between his legs onto the cracked wooden floorboards.

Archie does not sleep.

0332 HOURS

Chapter

4

Archie lies flat on his back, his head turned to the right, his left hand outstretched, his fingers splayed over his grandfather's Smith & Wesson .38/44 Outdoorsman. Bluing on metal, that looks almost black, attached to warm wood. The gun has a hard, carved handle with a checkered walnut diamond grip, polished from decades of use to a sheen, yet its ridges cut their shapes into his searching fingertips. Its cylinder juts out, the chambers creating the shape of a 3D S. A sight rises at the tip of the blue barrel, like a tidal wave facing back towards the gun's holder.

And it's loaded.

But not fully loaded.

Five of Pawpaw's precious hand-rolled store of bullets rest in the old gun's chambers; the remaining cache of bullets nestle in a box at the bottom of his cedar chest. Memories roll in like the waves of Lake Ontario onto the beach of his mind.

Pawpaw instructs Archie as he watches him chamber each hand-rolled round until he fills all but one chamber. "Be ready, son," he tells Archie, "and be safe. This old thing is faithful but has no safety mechanism. So we put it in with the way we load her up. Some say it's safer to be trained and ready than to rely on an empty chamber. I say both. You're not likely to shoot by accident when you're trained and in control, but you're a kid, Archie, better to reduce the risk."

Archie blinks his self back into the present. He remembers how his whole life up until then he knew Pawpaw chambered all six bullets and wonders what had decided him to increase the safety level. Archie never knew exactly why his grandfather had come around to a more modern sensibility when he'd first handed Archie his treasured Outdoorsman. Archie can hear Pawpaw as clearly as if he's standing beside him, the musky scent of sweat overriding the smell of gun oil, as the gun weighs heavy and awkward in his small hands. "Self-control, gun control, is the ultimate safety, son. Don't listen to those others who talk about safety, Archie. They think mechanisms and gizmos will keep them safe. No, it's your brain," he says, tapping his right temple as he bends his head to bore his blue eyes into Archie's innocent brown ones. And then he glances at the weapon, enormous in Archie's childish hands. Pawpaw frowns and glances back up at Archie's open, trusting face. Suddenly, Pawpaw whips the weapon from his hands, flips open the case, removes one bullet, closes the case, and spins it so that the empty chamber faces the barrel. He gives the gun back to Archie to hold. "Get used to its weight and its size, son," he instructs Archie as if he hasn't interrupted Archie's first lesson and contradicted what he'd just told him about safety. "Remember, son, your brain is the ultimate safety."

Pawpaw vanishes in the sound of a distant police siren. Archie is back on his well-used rooming-house bed.

Your brain, Archie thinks. *My brain,* he remembers. *My brain has kept me safe, will keep me safe. Yet Pawpaw's—*

No, he thrashes from side to side. *I don't want to remember, to think, to follow into the future where those memories and thoughts are taking me. Stop!*

Archie's sense of touch powers through his emotions to alert him to what his skin sensors are telling him. He is still touching the Smith & Wesson Outdoorsman. The cold metal of the gun under his fingertips overwhelms the grief of what he doesn't want to remember. The gun's battle-scarred metal soothes him, and his memories stop swapping the past for the present. The Outdoorsman lies there solid and reassuring; it speaks to him of history, of safety, of those days with Pawpaw when the man stood between him the boy and danger, when the man had taught him patiently, over and over, how to defend himself in the American way. The gun's bluing imprisons the memories in the past. Yet the antique's heft speaks them to him through his searching fingers.

Pawpaw had bought this gun...No, Pawpaw's father had given it to Pawpaw on his eighteenth birthday. A present for becoming a man who'd proven his worth on the family ranch. Pawpaw was the youngest and wouldn't inherit the ranch, but Pawpaw had told Archie that his daddy always said he had the best instinct for finding lost cattle and saving his father a bundle. In his great-grandfather's family, the youngest had been a worthy son, an economic boon. Pulling your own weight was important. It was everything. And his grandfather always did, from the time he'd finished grade school. *Maybe even before*, Archie thinks, as the memory of the man who'd lived close by, two blocks south and two blocks west of his parents and himself and his twin brother, loomed into view like a mountain range coming closer when driving toward it. Archie remembers his grandfather as a man who loomed, whose face spoke of living under the sun, his emotions unbeknownst to any man, hidden like the desert. An individual. A New Mexican by choice, a Texan by birth. A real American.

Pawpaw had ranged the vast lands of Texas, riding his horse, his gun holstered on his hip. He was a man's man, he often told Archie, a man who knew who he was and where he belonged right up until he left Texas to follow a woman to New Mexico.

"A woman will bring you down, lead you astray, be your nemesis," Pawpaw had told him the last day he'd seen him, "a gun will not. A woman will beguile you, make you do things you don't want to do, erase your manhood. But a gun will strengthen you. Don't let any woman do that to you, son. Choose your gun wisely and keep it by your side." Archie had listened politely; he'd learnt as a boy not to argue with his grandfather. It got a smack right across the face with an open hand. Archie involuntarily raises his free hand to touch his face, the memory of those smacks burning his unshaven skin. He cradles his right cheek in his right hand until the burning eases and all he remembers is Pawpaw's guttural laugh, that rare laugh that erupted whenever their collie bounced and skittered as motes danced in the hot air of the sun scorching their backyard.

Archie strokes the gun, his fingertips telling him about its nicks and hardness, its history of use and—

Archie's eyes shift to the digital clock's glow to watch its steady light until the numeral on the far right moves forward by one. He wants to remember Pawpaw as he was, a big, rangy man with thick, grey hair, spiky like his own once blonde-now-black hair. But Pawpaw's eyes were glacial blue. His are black in some lights, brown in others, as Sally had often said when she'd raise herself up on tip-toe to stare into his eyes.

Archie flips his head over to free himself from the memory.

He shoves the thoughts and feelings away as he retracts his hand from its home on the Outdoorsman. He doesn't let his hand lie under the white sheet and sleeping bag for long as he stretches his arm out again and feels beside the gun for his iPhone. He touches its plastic-covered edge, and the outdated smartphone sails off the other side of the nightstand. He grits his teeth against the vulgar language that lusts to spill out. Pawpaw had taught him self-control even in language. A real man keeps quiet. He doesn't display his emotions, not even anger or frustration. Archie yanks the sheet away from himself and slams his feet down on the floor, pain rocketing up his calves. He stands up, takes one step toward the window, and drops to his haunches. He feels around with tented fingers for his iPhone. His fingers land on the inside edge of the thick plastic cover. Like a projectile, the iPhone hurtles off of his fingers, slamming against the wall.

Archie lets out a yell. And bites his teeth together. He raises himself with the power of his abdominal muscles and thighs and stamps two steps over to the wall. He stares down at a slightly darker oblong in the oozing darkness at his feet.

Archie blinks as his jaw slackens.

The darkness solidifies. Archie snaps his mouth closed. He reaches down. Pain lances up his back, and he's thankful for the distraction of the physical pain that obliterates his psychic pain. He grabs the iPhone firmly in his hand and steps backwards until his bed hits the back of his knees, knocking him off balance and onto the bed. He touches the Home button with his left forefinger and presses down slightly. The phone springs to life. It buzzes in his hand. Siri waits for her command.

"Text David, are you awake?"

"OK," Siri chirps. "Here's your message to David. David, are you awake. Shall I send it?"

"Yes."

"Okay, your message is sent."

Archie presses the Home button to dismiss Siri and stares down at the black screen, feeling the molecules in the air pressing in on him, pushing him down into his emotions and memories escalating out of his cranium. "Pick up. Pick up." he whispers.

His iPhone pings a notification.

Relief floods Archie as he reads the first few lines of the message on his Lock Screen. With his left forefinger, he swipes the message right then presses down on the Home button briefly to unlock his iPhone and read the entire message.

"What's up, man? You can't sleep. Talk to me."

Archie likes David, a man who texts and never wavers from relationship.

He texts back: "Pawpaw."

"OK, man. That's bad. Brains again?"

"Yeah."

"You gotta talk to someone."

"No."

"Yes. And stop arguing with me, man. You know how it is. You know I'm right."

"I'm talking to you."

"A health professional, Archie."

"Don't use my name."

"It's not your real name, so what's the biggie. We all agreed we won't use your real name no more."

"Yeah."

Archie pauses, inhaling steadily and deeply, holding his breath in. David waits for him, doesn't bother him with texts about where he is, where he's gone, not like—

He controls his exhalation, feeling his heart slow to a softer rhythm. He's being paranoid, he knows it. The logical part of his brain, the one Sir—his father—had taught him to use, fires messages at him. David can use his name, for his name is attached to his Apple account and to his phone number. There is nothing new anyone can gain from hacking into his messages, and besides, they're using Signal. David had checked and triple-checked its security for him. He refused to quadruple-check the security protocols that the open source software uses to prevent NSA snooping into his messages. The VA can use his texts against him. That's what one of the men waiting to see their counsellor two years ago had told him. That's what they'd done to him. "Be careful," his fellow veteran had told him, "you don't know how they can twist your words, how they can make something innocent sound like you're a terrorist or wife beater." He'd found out later that that veteran had beaten his wife so badly she was in a coma in the intensive care unit of the local hospital; still, the man's words made sense to him then and today. The logical part of his brain tries to speak sense to him: *David isn't giving away any new information by using your name in the texts.*

Archie texts as he exhales: "Yeah. OK."

"Glad to hear it, man! Can you sleep now?"

"No."

"OK. What d'you need?"

"Company."

"You got it. You know it, man, any time, any time."

Archie smiles with his lips closed, and the skin around his eyes relaxes a mite. David knows how to write so that it sounds like he's speaking, though Archie has forgotten how David speaks. Archie texts back rapidly with his thumbs: "I know. Thanks."

"So whaddya want to talk about? The Mets?"

David knows how to rile me up, Archie grins to himself. *The Mets! No, I'm a Blue Jays fan. I came to Toronto, and I'm all in.* The Jays had won themselves a World Series, first time in over two decades, David and Andrew had told him. Nadine had blown a raspberry at their excitement, had told them real Canadians talk hockey. The men had groaned at her, and Andrew and David had argued through their blurring thumbs on phones over who was better, the Leafs or Canadiens. Archie still doesn't understand this hockey stuff; he likes baseball, the leisurely pace of the game, the way you can jaw your way through the innings while sipping a cold beer. Archie texts David: "The Mets are losers. No way winning a pennant."

David cheerfully argues with him, knowing that this will distract Archie until his sleepiness takes over, and he can sleep again. His plan works. Fifteen minutes into their conversation, Archie wiggles his butt backwards until his feet are elevated. Thirty minutes in, Archie slides around, shoves the pillow behind his back, and leans against the wall. Forty-five minutes in, Archie slips his legs underneath the top sheet and sleeping bag and over the next fifteen minutes, inch by inch, slouches down until he's lying flat on his back, his arms elevated in the air with his iPhone above his head, its screen staring down at him, his thumbs slowing down.

David texts him: "Hey man, you, me, first home game at the Dome in April. Now, go sleep."

"You got it," Archie texts back then presses down on the power button. His iPhone clicks off as he places it carefully on his nightstand. He pulls his arm back, forgetting to stroke his grandfather's gun, and turns on to his side, his back to the window, his body curled into himself.

Archie sleeps.

<u>0459 HOURS</u>

Chapter 5

IRRITATION CREEPS UP Archie's chest. Awareness flickers at the edges of his mind. Archie's eyes swivel side to side as he checks out his surroundings with his ears and the fine hairs erupting from his skin. Like little shards of glass, the irritation pricks the space inside his heart, urging him to get out. Get out where? Archie doesn't know. He's by himself, in a snug room—he darts his eyes to the right to sense the level of light on the door-side of his room while keeping his eyes closed—is his door open? No. It's pitch-black behind his eyelids. A vacuum of darkness that no light can penetrate. Archie tells himself to calm down. Relax, he thinks to the glass shards pricking, pricking, pricking him.

Get out.

Archie snaps open his eyes.

His ceiling glows amorphously above. Panic roils his digestive juices into his esophagus. Archie swallows hard, trying to suck saliva out of the dry-bed of his mouth. He sucks in his cheeks, urging his saliva glands to produce spit for him. He whispers to himself: "Relax,

relax, relax." Drops of saliva douse his cheeks and moisten his palate above his teeth, easing the stale gumminess. Again, he vacuums in his cheeks, but his glands won't give up any more precious liquid.

Archie swallows dryly, and panic rises into his heart.

He tears off the top bedsheet and vaults out of bed. Archie's sleeping bag flies off the bed and slides across the floor to land up against the multi-locked door in a crumpled heap. Tension rises his shoulders and drives his fingers into his hands. His short-clipped nails cut red lines into his palms. Archie had forgotten to clip them shorter last night, his nightly ritual to keep himself safe. But impending Remembrance Day ceremonies had consumed his thoughts so that he forgot even his routine functions.

"You're safe, you're safe, you're safe," Archie says loudly, over and over, hoping the repetition will make it so. "You're not," snarls a small voice that has more power than all the waterfalls in the world combined. Archie hears its threat; the potent voice squelches his soothing self-talk.

Archie's chin rears against his neck in his effort to swallow.

He flickers his tongue out, trying to wet his lips. He pulls his lips in and out, in and out, hoping that somewhere, somehow, his spit will gush into his desperate mouth and provide relief. It doesn't.

The VA counsellor's voice speaks to him from the distance of his memory banks: "When you feel that panic, Archie, tell yourself where you are, who you're with, that you're safe, what year it is." Archie blinks against that memory, wanting to hunch in on himself more than he wants to follow the advice of a man who'd left him.

No, his logical mind tries to tell him, *listen to his advice. Your counsellor didn't leave you. The VA made him leave you. He had no choice. A soldier must follow orders, even in hospitals.* "But why?" Archie moans to himself. Moisture beads his eyes and dots his thick, black lashes. He doesn't heed them. He crouches to the window. He splits the blinds open at the bent slat and peers out onto the night-blanketed street.

The street lays quiet.

Silver-metal streetlights light up the loneliness below his window. Windows in the dilapidated houses across from him are obsidian rectangles. *The devil's light*, he thinks. The devil doesn't like light that illuminates. The devil sucks suns into his belly and chews them up with the thousand mouths of the demons who reside in it.

Click.

Something clicked somewhere in his house. Suddenly, Archie drops onto his haunches, his back to the window, his head facing the door, his buttocks tensed, ready to spring him forward off his toes. His door stands in its place, unmoving. For long minutes Archie waits, watching. He sends his eyes around the perimeter of the door to check for changing light levels, for shadows moving stealthily in the concealing silence.

Nothing.

Archie sends his eyes around the perimeter of his room, over the walls blank of any artwork, over his bed, its top sheet half off it, over his nightstand—

The gun stops his scrutiny.

The Outdoorsman lies there, glinting in the artificial light slanting through the gap between the crooked blind slat and the one below it.

Archie's breath vibrates his vocal cords. The wheezing hum reverberates in the room. His eyes widen as he takes in the comforting sight. Archie straightens up gradually and glides over to his nightstand to stand over his gun with its long, blue-black barrel. The Outdoorsman lies there innocently on its left side. Carefully, he reaches his left hand down to pick up the gun. Archie holds it with his trigger finger along the length of the barrel, not slipping it into its natural place. He scans Pawpaw's hefty gun, the weight of it balanced and reassuring in his grip.

Archie relaxes.

The gun is his friend.

It was Pawpaw's friend.

"My Outdoorsman never leaves me," Pawpaw had told him one summer day, when the cicadas were quiet in the dry heat and the coyotes had found shade in the wadis to lie panting on their sides. The wildfire haze had obscured the far mountains as Pawpaw and he had sat on the front porch of his grandfather's home. That afternoon was one of the last times Archie had seen Pawpaw. Archie's father had had to help Pawpaw sell his home after his grandmother had died the previous year from congestive heart failure, a phrase his parents and grandparents had bandied about but meant nothing to him except that she always breathed heavily like a stuffy, old engine that belched stale smoke.

"Pawpaw can't live by himself." Sir's voice slices into Archie's hearing. "He's having trouble with his eyesight and feet. Diabetes." With his implacable tone, Sir concludes: "A nursing home is what he needs." Archie's father leaves to secure a spot.

Archie sits with Pawpaw. "They won't let me take this," Pawpaw says, patting his gun in its worn leather holster on his hip. "My trusty companion. It's with me always." Pawpaw's voice fades into another place, another time. Archie feels like Pawpaw has already left him. His heart staccatos nervously. He shuts his lips against words that want to spill out in case Pawpaw leaves him right then and there. He cannot conceive of a life without Pawpaw in it. Mortality was an abstract, not a reality.

"I want you to have it," Pawpaw says abruptly to Archie as he turns his head to stare right into Archie's soul with those eyes of his now faded from disease and the toll of aging but still glacial with hardness born from too much experience.

"Me?" Archie squeaks, intensely embarrassed at the high-pitched tone at odds with his normally smooth, deep voice.

"Yes, you. You're not a squeal like your twin. You're a man's man, like me. You're in the army, boy."

Archie has signed up and was on his way to basic training when he stopped in at his grandfather's for one last conversation. He talked to his grandfather nightly, just before suppertime. It was their ritual. He drove over in his beat-up Ford 150, its tan colour faded from its layers and layers of dust. Pawpaw shouted only minutes earlier, as he always had, as he watched Archie drive up: "The army will teach you to clean that up. Have some pride in yourself, boy!" Archie knows Pawpaw didn't want him to join the army. Gratitude lifts his lips, gratitude that Pawpaw accepts his decision and himself despite his inclination.

A faint bang, somewhere outside, jolts Archie. His consciousness shifts from the present of that long-ago New Mexican night into the present night of a chilly Toronto November. Archie is staring at his gun.

Archie thinks: *Pawpaw's companion, I'm holding it, as Pawpaw had held it that day.* The Outdoorsman's weight seems to lighten in his hand; Archie switches it into his right hand. Pawpaw was left-handed, but he's right-handed. Yet the gun doesn't seem to want to be held in his right hand; it demands to be switched back into his left.

Archie obeys.

The gun seems to come to life. The Smith & Wesson Outdoorsman—Pawpaw's gun—seems to be talking to him like Pawpaw is guiding him, urging him to do what he must do to escape. The shards of glass irritating his heart sharpen in their insistence that he must move, leave, get out, just go. Now!

Archie lifts the gun higher until it's hovering right before his eyes. His left forefinger slides into its accustomed place on the trigger. He feels the impending effort of pulling that trigger. He extends his left arm out while keeping the gun's profile at his eye level.

Archie stands there for long minutes. The glowing numerals on his clock change upward from 04:33 to 04:34 to 04:35. The numerals crawl into his attention. His eyes focus on the last numeral as it changes from 5 to 6. He refocuses on his gun. Archie bends his wrist towards his face, and the barrel of the gun rotates toward his eyes, towards the space between his eyes. His hand freezes. The gun is pointing to the side right of his right eye. He tenses his trigger finger. If he shoots now, he'll graze his temple, the tender point of his head. But he won't die.

And he really wants to leave.

To escape.

To not be here with its moments of sudden prickling deep inside him, of sounds that throw him down into vigilance, into the unabated loneliness of his family that had loved him so much that they'd told him—

Archie judders his head free of that memory. He wants to hurl up the horrors, to purge their evil. But he cannot. Pawpaw's gun can take him away from it all. His faithful companion, Pawpaw had said, the evening before his companion had not let him down. The night it had let him escape. Archie angles his wrist ninety degrees, the flexion straining his muscles and tendons, and draws his arm backwards. The .38/44 moves its sight toward his left temple.

"You're going to be there, right, Archie?" Andrew's voice booms out of nowhere.

Memory becomes reality.

"Promise me, Archie. You'll be there?"

Archie had nodded.

"Not a nod, Specialist," Andrew had commanded. "I want an affirmative, Specialist."

"Affirmative, sir."

"Good," Andrew had slapped him on the back. "We'll be in the parade. You don't have to be, but I want to see you near that cenotaph."

Archie had nodded.

Andrew had stared right into his skull. "I want to hear you say it, Specialist."

Archie had said: "I will be there, sir, right next to the cenotaph, saluting you as you march by."

"Good man," Andrew had replied warmly, gripping his shoulder with his large warm hand for an instant.

Archie's view of the gun blurs as he lowers it down and places it back onto the nightstand soundlessly.

He had promised.

Weariness covers Archie like a sodden blanket as his wrist throbs from its unwilling bend under a tortured mind's will.

Archie drops onto his bed, his head into his hands, and sobs silently, not wanting to wake up his rooming-house neighbour, not wanting to hear any more pounding of shells and fists, not wanting to live in abandonment's stink any more.

0600 HOURS

Chapter 6

THE BUGLE LIFTS Archie straight up into the air and onto his feet, back ramrod straight, arms clamped to his sides. The bugle repeats its tune, and Archie's eyes flutter. He'd fallen back asleep only five minutes ago, he's sure. Dawn already? The bugle trumpets, "Wake up!" again. Archie squints yet stays at attention. The bugle doesn't stop, and if anything, its volume grows as if the bugle is moving towards him from below his chin. Archie's brows draw together imperceptibly. The din jangles his nerves. Darkness keeps its hold on his room, although there seems to be a relaxing of the evil of the night, a bit of hope reflected in the dawn filtering through the metal slats of his blinds. Archie sends his eyes around the room; he gathers into his awareness what he can see, hear, and smell from his at-attention stance next to his bed. What were black shapes in the night only minutes ago emerge out of the gloom as recognized furniture. No sweet-sour smell of drunken breath nearby.

Archie relaxes his neck and looks down, scanning the nightstand then the floor back to the nightstand, puzzled, for the bugle is screaming from below him and to his left. His iPhone is ringing.

Archie snatches it up, presses the green phone icon: "Archie!" he barks.

"Andrew here, Archie. How are you?"

"I'm well, sir," Archie barks.

"Stand down, Specialist. You're not on parade."

"Yes, sir," Archie replies in more modulated tones as banging commences from the other side of his wall, making his bed slide back and forth rhythmically. Archie swivels, bends his knees, and relaxes, falling straight down to sit on his bed, halting the bed's annoying movement. "Just a sec, sir."

Andrew's silent waiting hushes the phone line, as Archie steadies his breathing into slower and slower inhales and exhales. His mind flows into his lungs. Only his arm holding up his iPhone stays tense for fear the phone will fall out of his hand.

"Archie?" queries a slightly nervous voice on the other end of his iPhone that he still has clamped to his ear.

"Here, sir," Archie replies, returning to exterior awareness, relieved the banging has stopped. His neighbour is too tired to shout.

"How are you, Archie?"

"Fine, sir," Archie says in his deep tones.

"Good man. Had a good night?"

"No."

"That's to be expected. Glad you're here."

"I keep my promises, sir."

"I know. You're a good soldier. I'm glad to call you a member of our team."

"Thank you, sir."

"Are you ready for today?"

"Not yet, sir."

"You will be?"

Archie pauses. He's not sure. He'd promised Andrew he'd be here, still present, still breathing, in the morning. Had he promised he'd show up for Remembrance Day? Archie's brow furrows; confusion clouds his eyes. Memory skips away. He hates he can't remember. He tries not to think about these gaps. But right now, right here with Andrew waiting for him to answer, he must remember. But...

Archie stifles his dismay. No, he cannot remember. Panic hollers, echoes in his skull; he thrusts the panic away. A soldier does not panic. A well-trained soldier knows how to think on his feet, to be agile when he doesn't have all the pieces and equipment together, to make do with what he has, and to work with others to make an effective singular fighting unit. That's what the Canadians had taught him on Afghanistan's harsh training ground. He came up here to join them, the agile, thinking ones.

"I...," Archie falters.

"Remembrance Day is important, Archie. We're counting on you to join us at the Cenotaph. We're a team; we can't be a team if you're not there." Andrew waits a moment. "You're part of our unit, Specialist. An essential part."

Archie fixates on the blinds. "I understand, sir."

"Nadine is depending upon you."

"I won't let her down," Archie's deep voice softens. The thought of her quells the panic.

"I know you won't, Specialist. We all appreciate you travelling up here to join us. We weren't quite a team until you came. You're a valued member, Archie."

"Thank you, sir."

"We'll expect you at the Cenotaph at ten hundred hours."

Archie's head jerks. No, no, no.

"Archie?" Andrew asks after the pause grows too long. "You okay?"

"I can't do crowds, sir."

"I know, Specialist. And I wouldn't ask it of you for any other day, any other event. But this one's important. We'll all be there. We're going there for our friends and our fallen heroes, the ones we left behind. We owe it to them to remember them."

"Yes, sir," Archie answers, resignation weakening his voice. Archie's head drops; his body slouches. He cannot refuse duty. Pawpaw had instilled in him what being a man was all about, regarded him higher than his twin because he was a real man, and men understand duty. Archie came here because his Canadian brothers-in-arms understood duty and honour better than any other soldier or officer he'd served under. Canada is home. He's liked here, respected here...wanted here. Archie straightens his spine. The least he can do is remember them, the Canadians and Americans who'd lost their lives serving for freedom and country.

Andrew's breathing becomes audible on the other end of the line, but Andrew says nothing. Archie appreciates that. His old commanding officer wanted subordinates to reply right away, to never let a silence gather. But Andrew is different; he's relaxed like the Canadians were in that desert hell of Afghanistan. They'd talk calmly, friendly like to the locals. They never rushed them; they stood there, legs apart, arms and hands resting on their weapons as if they had all the time in the world. Not like his commanding officer in the US Army. With him, talk had to be sharp and quick. Marching had to be double time. Keep up with the LAVs else get left behind. Floor the convoy truck else have him yelling right in your ear: "Gun it, soldier. What you waiting for? The Tal-i-ban to come up your ass and shoot it off. We're not a bunch of old ladies here. We're men fighting a real war. Get the lead out, or I'll shove you out!"

"Archie?" Andrew calls Archie back in his calm, assuring authoritative voice.

But Archie's consciousness remains firmly on that Afghan road, himself in the truck driver's seat, his commanding officer's voice hoarse from shouting over the revving roar of the engine that rumbles his brain.

"Archie!" Andrew booms.

Archie slingshots back into the Toronto dawn, sees the rough, age-blackened oak boards underneath his bare feet. He blinks rapidly, trying to orient himself.

Andrew says: "Archie. It's Remembrance Day. Are you with us?"

"Yes, sir," Archie says quietly.

"Don't be ashamed, Specialist, it happens to the best of us."

"Yes, sir."

"Now where were we? Oh yeah, Cenotaph. Ten hundred hours."

"I…"

"I know, the crowds. You got that thing I gave you?"

"Yes, sir."

"You learnt how to use it yet?"

"Yes, sir."

"Tell me."

Archie opens and closes his mouth like a fish in air. He reaches forward and pulls the lone drawer of his nightstand open and stares at the little black box with its black wires snaking and curling into each other with their long clips on their ends, one red, one black. He'd tried it like Andrew had told him to. The device had worked. It'd been like those drugs his primary care physician had given him, except all that had happened with this device was he'd felt less stressed. No dry mouth, no blue feet. Just less stressed. But Archie isn't sure about a device that uses electricity to ease his anxiety, even if it's battery-powered electricity. Pills he understands.

"It's like you're wearing super cool earbuds."

"I suppose," Archie says cautiously, all military hierarchy lost to him, as his nervousness takes hold.

"You see your health as important, right? We take care of our bodies, including you. You're an inspiration to the team, Archie. This is one more weapon in your arsenal, Specialist. Just one more weapon. Okay?"

Archie breathes in through his nostrils the cool molecules of the November air. "Yes, sir. I understand, sir." Archie reaches in and pulls out the little black box, its wires dangling from between his fingers, and lays it down in front of the barrel of his best friend.

"You'll wear it. You'll feel better. And the crowds won't bother you," Andrew pauses. "As much."

Silence.

"You can do this, Archie. Nadine needs you there. She's having a rough time."

Archie sits up, alert. "Ex-boyfriend?"

"Yes. He's bothering her."

"Didn't she get a restraining order?"

"Yes, yes, she did. But you know the civvies. They don't know real danger when they see it. It's up to us to head off the danger. Understand?"

Archie's back quivers. His head lifts, his eyes tighten as he looks straight ahead, planning on how to address the threat. "Yes, sir, I understand, sir."

"Good man. We'll be marching in the parade. But we'll be looking for you. You're our touchstone, the one who will ground us as we remember them, the fallen, our friends and brothers and sisters. We never forget."

"No sir, you Canadians don't. I admire that about you guys. It's why I came up here. Never forget, not even the..."

"It's okay, Archie. We know," Andrew says in an even, low tempo, like a man to his rescued anxious-ridden dog, his best mate and friend. In stronger tones, he continues: "Alright then. We'll see you when we march past the Cenotaph. After the two minutes of silence, we'll gather at Nathan Phillips Square. You remember the corner?"

"I do."

"Good. Glad you're with us, Archie."

Archie can't get himself to say, "So am I." He settles for: "Thanks."

They disconnect their call. Archie lets his arm drop. Sleeplessness weighs on his arms, his hands, his chest, his legs, even his feet. His feet hurt as they sit there on the floor, unmoving. He slowly puts his iPhone face down on the nightstand next to...Archie averts his eyes. He'd best leave it behind.

0700 HOURS

Chapter
7

Archie has survived the hostile night; the dangers of the day greet him. Archie's nose twitches. Commuters blow exhaust through his thin windows. Archie had fallen back asleep in seconds after Andrew's call. He knows it's 0700 hours without having to look at the accusing clock. The morning feels have begun. Stiffness aches his joints; spasms frozen by sleep pain his muscles. Archie slits his eyelids open and stretches his neck, his shoulders, his legs, and hips until the spaces between his bones crack their acquiescence. Archie relieves them all and, with one contraction of his abdominal muscles, sits up and swings his legs out from between his sheets and over the side of the bed. Fatigue washes over him. He stalls. His hands fist against the bed, on either side of his thighs, to prop him until his will regains momentum, and he pushes himself up to standing. He sways. He rubs his face violently with both hands, willing himself to wake up.

Archie doesn't want to be awake.

He doesn't want to be here.

He wants to be...somewhere else. Somewhere where there's no pain, no rejection, and no violence. Archie drags his hands down off his chin and drops them suddenly to his side. He exists. Today he is here. Archie had promised Andrew he'd show up at the Remembrance Day parade, and he's a man of his word. Pawpaw's words ring down the years: "Count on your gun, and let others count on your word."

Archie glances at his nightstand and spots the little black box. Archie's mouth turns down, and he shifts his gaze to his Outdoorsman, its heavy length a testament to its faithful service to Pawpaw. If only...it had been faithful to him last night...this morning. Early, early this morning. But it had not. And now he must put it away. Archie's strong fingers wrap around it for a moment before he pushes out the cylinder holding the bullets in its chambers. He upends the gun, and the bullets Pawpaw had hand-rolled so patiently in the sunsetting hours of his last night fall into Archie's open, waiting hand. His fingers close over the five bullets; his eyes squeeze shut against the impetus to reload the chambers. *Put the bullets away*, he instructs himself.

Carrying both bullets and gun, Archie takes three stealthy steps over to his cedar chest. Archie pushes the cylinder back into place and lays the gun down on the bed on its side. He lifts the lid of the chest with his free right hand until it's high enough to stay open on its own. He digs deep through the boxes and papers that are piled on the right side of the chest until his hand touches the worn, white, thick-cardboard box that holds Pawpaw's bullets. Archie pulls it up and places it next to the gun. He shimmies open the lid and carefully places the bullets back in between their brothers, breathing in the familiar smell, like fresh fireworks not yet released. With both hands, Archie eases the lid closed and the box down through several piles of paper in the chest to nestle between other boxes he'd rather not think about.

But Archie does.

For his hand touches one of them.

Archie cannot resist. He pulls it up toward him, removes its lid, and stares at the medal with its ribbon nestled inside. Expressionlessly, he replaces the lid and pushes the box back down between all the papers until it's beside the box of bullets. He rearranges the papers until they look undisturbed, as if their piles extend to the bottom of the chest. Archie's feet walk him around the chest, and he drops down to lay flat on the floor. He reaches underneath the low bed and carefully, so as to make no sound, pulls out the heavy safe sitting on its own little carpet. He punches in the combination code, opens its door, reaches up to the top of the bed, and with great care, places Pawpaw's companion in it. Archie shuts the safe door, relocks the safe, and pushes it on its carpet soundlessly back into its barely hidden place under the bed. *At least the vets who live in this rooming house will never figure out how to unlock it,* Archie smiles cheerlessly to himself.

Archie pulls out an army-green towel from the left side of the chest and flips the towel over his shoulder while closing the chest's lid. He retrieves his keys from his nightstand and steps to his dresser. He opens his top dresser drawer and pulls out his underwear, T-shirt, dress shirt, and pants for the day. He picks up a tea towel to lay his clothes on and a large steel bowl, walks to the door, and slips on flip-flops that await him beside the door. A grimace twists his face as he steels himself. Archie leans towards the door and places his left ear against it. Nothing, no sound. No one but he is awake at this hour. Archie unlocks all five locks and drags in breath. He yanks open the door on its oiled hinges, locks it behind himself, and marches down to the latrine. *Bathroom,* he reminds himself. Archie pushes the nicotine-stained door open, its round metal handle loose in his hand and useless. As he steps into the tiny space cockroaches call home, he empties his mind of all thoughts, his body of all sensations, his eyes of all visuals as he does his business, scrubs himself clean in the shower, and dresses. Hot water steams the bowl, and he carries it back to his room. He unlocks his door, enters, slips off his flip-flops, and places the bowl on the dresser. He quickly turns back to the door to lock all five locks.

Archie shaves using the small mirror the army had given him. The shared bathroom with its cracked sink, its mouldy shower tub, its stained walls, and flickering fluorescent light repels him. He won't risk cutting himself in there. The hard-shelled black and brown and grey multi-legged creatures that scurry toward his feet would feast on him.

The feeling of many feet, of a dragging tail moving over his arms, lifts the hair on his skin. Archie stops shaving and stares at his arms in their ironed shirt, at his legs in their pant legs with their sharp folds. Nothing. Memory. He stares and stares until the memory and sensation retreat from the sharp visual of reality.

He finishes shaving.

He leaves his bowl where it is and turns on his hotplate. A small fridge sits beside his dresser and Archie opens it to retrieve eggs, his half-empty bread bag, and bacon. Not Canadian bacon. He couldn't get used to that taste. And no maple syrup either. He makes a moue of distaste at the remembered first morning when his commanding officer, Andrew, and his unit had poured maple syrup on their bacon. It had been a rare treat trucked in in honour of their new American embedded soldier. His new Sergeant had poured the amber, sticky liquid over Archie's eggs before he could stop her. He'd taken one bite, and his lips had drawn back at the sweetness. The Canadians had laughed and laughed, then mopped up every drop of syrup with the last bite of scrambled eggs. Later, Andrew had introduced him to the British fry-up, a cultural remnant from his British grandmother, he'd told Archie: bacon fried first, then eggs in the bacon fat, followed by sliced tomatoes, and last a slice of bread. Their cook had learnt how to make it to Andrew's liking, even with its dusting of sand in each bite.

When he'd arrived in Toronto, Archie had determined to leave his past behind, including the food of his youth. The fry-up was decent. He could tolerate that.

Archie waits till the hot plate has heated his small fry pan before laying down in it the rashers of bacon side by side, from one edge of the pan to the other. He likes them crisp. As the strips of cured pig meat hiss and spit, he retrieves a plate from the bottom dresser drawer, along with a roll of paper towel. He rips one sheet off the roll and puts the roll back. He lifts the bacon out and onto the paper towel-covered plate. He cracks two eggs into his pan and fries them until their edges are golden and crisp. He places the eggs with their lacy whites on top of the bacon. He extracts a slice of white bread out from its bag and drops it into the pan. He slips the paper towel out from under the bacon, folding it in a square and inserting it into the bread bag to re-use later. He returns the bag to the fridge. Archie flips the bread and fries the other side until it's bronzed with heat and soaked-up grease. He grabs the pan's handle and shakes the bread to lie beside the eggs and bacon. He restores the pan back to the hot plate and turns the dial to off.

Archie carries his breakfast over to the table and sits down. He stares down at his plate, expressionlessly. The plate of eggs, bacon, and fried bread is missing colour. Brown, white, and yellow have no punch, none of the heat he loves. Sighing at his inability to shed his past, he pushes his chair back and returns to the dresser. Archie drops to his haunches, opens the bottom drawer of the dresser, and reaches to its far right corner. He pulls out a jar of chile. Red and green. Christmas. It's the last jar of the several of her homemade chile Ma had hastily placed in his kit as he headed out the door for Canada. It's old. *Is it still safe?* Archie shrugs. Standing up in one smooth movement, he pushes the drawer closed with his right foot and walks back to the table, unscrewing the jar's lid with a satisfying pop. He forks out one red and one green chile. His brain craves half the jar; his discipline, his need for control reseals the jar. He eats his fry-up quickly, cutting up huge pieces of egg and bacon with tiny slices of chili to fork onto one-quarter of the fried bread to shove into his mouth and chew rapidly and competently, trying not to miss the spicy staples of his New Mexican life. He doesn't choke once on the mound of food that stuffs his cheeks.

Breakfast isn't fiery enough.

Archie cleans up. He wants to leave the plate and his knife and fork where they are. But a sudden movement catching his eye from the far corner of his room discourages such indolence. Archie goes back to the bathroom to empty the bowl and refill it with hot, clean water. Back in his room, he washes all his dishes, dries them, and puts them away. He leaves the bowl where it is. Maybe a few roaches will drown in the soapy, oily water.

And now to duty.

Archie pulls open his top dresser drawer and takes out a pair of green socks. He pulls open the second drawer and takes out his boot polishing kit. Today, he will do a proper spit polish on his boots. They're well used, the leather creased all across his toes, but a spit polish will bring up the shine, make the creases not so bad. He picks up his boots and carries them and the polishing kit back to his bed.

Archie sits down on his bed and opens the can of polish. He takes the rag and with a finger inserted in the rag scoops up black polish. He lifts one boot up in his left hand and, with his right, circles polish on his boot with sure swiftness. He spits. Saliva globs on the polish. He circles it into the black polish over the toe of his boot, round and round and round, until the leather in that small spot shines. He repeats the action over the rest of the boot and on his other boot: polish, spit, polish.

Archie lays down his second finished boot next to the first one, satisfied. One thing the US Army had taught him: how to care for his boots, how to bring up the shine, and how to look sharp.

Archie reaches underneath the mattress he's sitting on and pulls out his Sig Sauer P320. His hand easily clasps the iron weight of the weapon with its polymer plastic grip foundation underneath the smooth metal of the grey-black slide with its length-long edges. The weapon's menacing rail of width-wide ties at the bottom front of the grip module is empty, in combat mode. Archie had cleaned it last night, as he always does. His trigger finger lies flat along the elongated trigger guard. He places it next to his hip on the bed in order to pull on and lace up his boots.

Archie rechecks his boots' shine and straightens his cuffs over them before picking up his Sig Sauer, pointing it down to the floor, his finger naturally alongside the trigger guard, not crooked around the trigger. He stands and carries his ever-present defence over to his chest and lays it down on top of the bottom of the bed. Again, Archie slides his safe out from under the bed. Again, he unlocks it and opens its small, heavy door and pulls out a black metal magazine, heavy with the weight of ten bullets—he'd taken out the extra seven New Mexico law allows in the magazine since he'd wanted to adapt to the Canadian way—to a point—and lays it on the bed. He relocks the safe and pushes it on its carpet back into its place. He lifts the lid of his chest and reaches down to the bottom of the chest, groping underneath the piles of towels and sheets, and pulls out his leather concealed carry case. He shuts the lid of the chest and picks up the magazine. With the palm of his hand supporting the base of the magazine, he slides it with even pressure up into the handle of his Sig, locking it home with a fat click. Archie lifts and sights the gun, lining up the forward white dot between the two rear white dots. He racks the action: he places his left hand over the front of the muzzle, the lacerations on either side of the slide digging familiarly into his palm and fingers, and pulls the slide backward. A bullet loads, and the slide glides forward back into the closed position. Archie hooks his concealed carry case into his belt and stuffs the case into his left pocket. He slides his combat weapon into it so that the grip and the bottom of the handle are facing toward his right hand but it's invisible once he puts his jacket on.

Secure, he strides over to the three pegs that he'd drilled into the wall next to the door. On one hangs his dress jacket on its hanger, the ether-like odour from the dry cleaning still clinging to it. The smell of clean bolsters him. Archie slides the jacket off the hanger and slides it up his arms and over his shoulders. He buttons it up with one hand, then pulls down the hem with both hands to smooth it over his chest and hips. He unhooks the waterproof and insulated outdoor army jacket that Andrew had given him from its peg next to the door and buttons it up. Last, he takes the khaki Tilley Hat from off its peg and places it on his head. He adjusts its brim with both hands so that the fabric is not crooked and it shades his eyes. He's not used to November damp yet; but he doesn't mind it. This is the life he chose; this is the life he wants if he must resist Medusa's song of escape. Archie takes one last look round his room. All is clean. Nothing is out. He glances down at his left hip. Nothing is visible.

Archie unlocks his door, exits, and locks all his locks with three keys.

Archie departs the rooming house in search of coffee.

<u>0800 HOURS</u>

Chapter 8

ARCHIE PUSHES OPEN the door of his coffee home, The Rest Shtop, and enters warmth that embraces him with aromas of brewing coffee and strawberry danishes, sounds of hissing steam jetted from a frother, and murmurings of satiated people.

"Hey, how are you? The usual?" the barista calls, poking his head out from behind his magical machine.

"Yes," Archie replies, walking up to the counter.

"It's on the house. And a—"

"No need. I can pay."

"We have this argument every year. I insist. You say no. I say yes. And who wins?" the barista grins, his teeth flashing good humour, his eyes challenging yet sharing a laugh, as he twists the knob to release richly aromatic espresso into a tiny glass cup.

Archie smiles, "You do," as the barista turns to the brewer on the wall counter, slips a large paper coffee cup under the nozzle, presses down on the lever above, and pours a cup of steaming coffee for Archie.

"That's right. So why don't we say, 'You get coffee on the house and a doughnut?'"

"Alright." Archie dips his head in good grace at giving in. The barista hands him a steaming cup of coffee along with a napkin and the doughnut in its bag that had been readied a minute before Archie had arrived. Archie walks them over to the counter against the window. He reaches into his upper right-hand jacket pocket and retrieves the ziplock plastic bag filled with brown-plastic pill bottles he stores there. He twists off one cap at a time and doles out one at a time into his hand a pill, a vitamin, an anti-oxidant, extracts, and energy builders, swallowing each with a gulp of hot, strong coffee. Finished, he recaps all the bottles, slips them back into the well-used bag, presses his fingers over its top, zips it closed, folds over the top, and pushes the bag back into his pocket, its home.

Archie leans forward, elbows on the counter, and sips the rest of the coffee as it cools in between the four bites it takes for him to eat his doughnut. He cannot taste the cinnamon sugar coating, neither the zing of the spice nor the caramel sweetness of the organic sugar. He wipes his hands with the napkin and contemplates the passing parade of people hurrying to work, heads down against the drizzle that suddenly spurts from the flat, grey sky. Umbrellas pop open, and walking turns to half jogging.

Archie lets his mind fill up with the people that he sees, the brake-and-hasten driving he notices, the sidewalks he watches darken under the onslaught of the quickening rain. The visual obliterates the emotional and the memories that arrive every morning dragging in their emotions fresh as if they're new, current, and hadn't visited him before.

Archie sighs, slips off his stool, and walks over to the trash bin and tosses in his cup, crumpled napkin, and empty bag.

"Bye!" the barista calls out. Archie looks towards him and nods as the man adds: "And thank you for your sacrifice."

More than you know, more than you know, Archie thinks as he pushes open The Rest Shtop's glass door and breathes in the pelting rain. He strides rapidly down the street to St. James Cathedral and steps into the shelter of its open doors. He listens to the beat of the heavens for a minute before fishing his iPhone from out of his left-hand pocket and launching Signal video call. Andrew's mug appears on his display.

"Good to see you, Archie," he booms, meaning it literally.

Archie nods; the visual call means he doesn't have to talk. Not talking suits him.

"You all set, Archie?"

Archie nods again. This time Andrew waits. Archie's commanding officer is compassionate but unrelenting. Andrew wants a verbal answer. He knows Archie can do it, and so he waits because he doesn't want Archie to deteriorate further. Archie knows this. Each time, he thinks he really can't speak. Each time, he resents Andrew waiting for him to verbalize thoughts. Each time, he questions to himself why Andrew does this to him. And then finally he acquiesces. "Yes sir," Archie replies.

"Good man. If we don't see you in the crowd—" Archie frowns. Andrew changes tack. "You got that assistive device on you?"

"No."

"Go back to get it."

Archie replies with silence. He leaves his room in the morning and returns at night. It's his way, his routine. Returning between those hours is not his way.

Andrew's voice takes on a commanding tone: "We need you there. Nadine is counting on us."

"I know, sir. Her ex paid me a visit."

"When?" Andrew interrogates.

"Early this morning."

"What happened?"

"I got rid of him."

"Why did he come?"

"He thought I was having an affair with Nadine."

Andrew sighs and looks off the screen to the left unseeingly. "Well…," he muses, "Hopefully he won't return."

"He will."

Andrew looks back through the screen into his eyes. "What will you do?"

"I don't know."

"You carrying?"

"Yes," Archie replies expressionlessly. Archie may be in Canada, but he's an American. And he's got a mission. It's his story.

Andrew stares into his eyes for a long minute. Archie returns the look without a twitch. He feels nothing, anyway. Andrew is the first to look away. He thinks for a moment. "Alright. You think he'll return?"

"I do."

"What do you think he'll do?"

"He tried to break down my door. I took care of him."

"Is he hurt?"

"Only his ego."

"That means he'll be like a pit bull with a toy poodle in his mouth."

"Yes, sir."

"We can handle him. But it's Nadine I'm worried about."

"Why?" Archie wrinkles up his eyebrows. The first sign of emotion. "She can handle herself. I saw her take down a man twice her size and height, no sweat."

"This isn't Afghanistan."

"So? He's smaller than the men she dealt with there."

"That's as may be. But she's not protecting anyone, not fighting for her country."

"That shouldn't matter."

"It does."

"She's fighting for herself. That matters."

"You would think so. But women are…"

"Pawpaw used to say you couldn't trust women."

"He was wrong."

Archie's mouth tightens. Pawpaw cannot be declared wrong, especially as doubt had crept into him these last few months about his grandfather's philosophy, about his teachings, about his action. He doesn't want to face his doubts, though, nor think how he'd trusted Nadine in the field and depended on her confident, cheerful presence. He suddenly wants to press the red phone receiver icon. But he's done that before and found Andrew in his face minutes later blasting him. It's better to stay on the phone, no matter how much the rising tide of panic and anger impels him to run. He resists. Andrew narrows his eyes slightly. And then deliberately relaxes them so that they look wide open, unthreatening. "Nadine is complicated. She needs our help."

"She has mine."

Andrew nods. "Good. She has all of ours. We just need to be prepared."

"Always."

Andrew lets that go. He checks the time at the top of his smart phone's display and knows Archie has as well. Morning prayer will start soon in the cathedral. He doesn't know why Archie goes but does know it's sacrosanct. Archie likes his morning routine, and not even Remembrance Day preparations may interrupt it.

"If we don't see you in the march past, we'll meet at Nathan Phillips Square. Usual place."

"Yes, sir. Thank you, sir." Archie refrains from saluting reflexively before pressing the red receiver icon. He swivels on his toes, removing his hat, and walks in to hushed St. James Cathedral, his boots ringing on the floor and heart finding peace in the familiar fragrances of wood polish and well-worn books that envelop him, to sit in his accustomed folding chair at the back of the east side aisle's sunlit Lady Chapel.

Chapter
9

ARCHIE EMERGES FROM the Cathedral and shelters underneath the repeating carved-stone arches of its entrance. Leaden clouds grace the sky and pour out their misery on the greyed streets below with their grooves of streetcar tracks. Cars hiss by, throwing up walls of dirty water at pedestrians approaching the intersection of King and Church. Some don't hop out of the way, blinded by their umbrellas that they're holding forward to guard them against the wind and sky water. Archie hauls his khaki-coloured Tilley hat out of his jacket's cavernous bottom right-hand pocket. With both hands, he pulls it down over his head and neatens the brim. Archie pulls up his collar and hunches his shoulders as he leaves the safety of the vaulted entrance and enters the downpour. Rain charges the surrounding air, drumming on his brim, and washes the streets, cleansing them of oil, gasoline, litter, and all the detritus of humans. Un-soldier-like, he stuffs his hands into his jacket's slit pockets behind its outer pockets and strides south towards Lake Ontario, the mighty body of water that anchors the city along its southern edge and, on hot days, has a slightly seaweed-and-fishy odour.

Water. After the desert and heat of Afghanistan, after the vast distances of sun-dried landscapes of his home state, Toronto with its lake of many moods and dangerous ocean-like behaviour refreshes him. It quenches his thirst for escape, for succour, for renewal. Rain will energize the waves and sluice the odours, Archie hopes as he hastens southward.

Archie strides around pedestrians blinded by umbrellas to oncoming people. He steps out of the way of cyclists pedalling on the sidewalk, weaving between old and young, keeping a safe distance from the drivers speeding and lane changing their way to work. He swerves around strollers covered in plastic domes and doesn't miss a pace in his mission to get to the water. He turns left at the Esplanade and walks swiftly through intersections where cars wait impatiently for their lights to turn green. Archie keeps walking east through a social housing neighbourhood, the like of which he'd not seen until he'd arrived in Toronto. During Archie's welcoming tour, Andrew had described the St. Lawrence neighbourhood as ground-breaking for its day; this social housing initiative was clearly a point of pride for Andrew, who felt the obligation to look after battle-scarred men and women extending into the state's obligation for taking care of its needy. *This is who Andrew is,* Archie thinks as he raises his head and scans the attractive housing, its greenery now flattened underneath November's dripping cold.

Archie lowers his head again and watches his black booted feet pound out the one-two rhythm as he heads toward the Distillery District. His hands remove themselves from his pockets almost subconsciously to keep strident time with his feet. His feet angle him automatically toward the path that runs alongside a large fenced green space, currently a landscape of mud and flattened browning grass. The rain eases its onslaught, and Archie lifts his head to feel the diminishing lashing of cold drops against his tanned face. The steady pinging sends up electrical signals throughout his skin, eliciting answering signals deep within him. *I'm a soldier, I've fought many battles. I've been in firefights, driven long distances along tracks that're merely beaten ribbons in the landscape. I've walked and driven for hours and hours with IEDs threatening to explode underneath me at any moment. Imminent mortality; imminent loss of legs or arms.*

I fought well, Archie mouths.

I have that medal in my chest to prove it.

I hate it.

Archie's lips draw back in disgust, for the medal speaks to him of the friends he supposedly saved and what he had to do to survive the US Army's 5th Combat Brigade Team. Archie commands himself to ignore the rain that suddenly feels like fingers flicking his face and to ignore the answering irritation within himself. He strides forward faster, trying to out-walk, out-soldier the irritation whose purpose seems to be to enrage him. He flies out of the fenced-off path onto the concrete sidewalk and onto the road. Archie cannot halt his momentum. Cars blast horns and brake, skidding on the road's water film. Archie senses a red car coming at him, stains of rain meandering like blood spatter across its hood; its hood plunges in the driver's adrenaline-fuelled stomping of his brakes. Wiper blades swoosh across the windshield in their steady back-and-forth, back-and-forth. Archie watches the front wheels as the car skids right up to his legs. His mind and heart blank. The car stops with barely a whisper against his pants.

Tingling crawls across Archie's cheeks, pulling his gaze up towards the driver, his torso twisting at the hips to follow suit. Anger contorts the driver's face. Suddenly, the man's face dissolves into horror. The window whirs down, and the driver sticks his head out. "I'm sorry, man. I almost hit you. You survive over there, and I almost hit you. I'm sorry, I'm sorry."

Archie blinks back into consciousness. He stuffs his hands back into his pockets. Canadians. Archie's heard sorry so many times in his walks around the city, but this one…Archie shakes his head ruefully. He cannot believe it. He's at fault in his heedless escape from the irritation within him, and this man is sorry? Archie opens his mouth, but no words come. The man is telling him he's grateful for what he's done for his country. Did Archie do it for Canada? For his own country, America? Or did he do it for himself? Archie's not sure. It's Remembrance Day, and he doesn't want to remember that long-ago day on his eighteenth birthday when he'd left his house and his mother's shouted "happy birthdays" and his father's "you're a man now, time to act like one" behind and beelined to the local US Army office to enlist. He'd exchanged an artificially cold house, its kitchen emanating chili spice and vanilla sweetness, for an echoing sterile building redolent of floor cleaner, hoping military regimen would take him farther away. He didn't care where he trained, where he shipped out. The only family he'd miss was Pawpaw. When Pawpaw had left his birthday party, extra slices of birthday cake in hand for later, Archie had taken it as his cue to leave for the enlistment office. He'd take care of figuring out how he and his grandfather would keep in touch. He had had plans, so many plans, about how he was going to buy Pawpaw a computer, how he was going to teach him how to use email, how he and his father would—

A horn blast. A shout, "He's a veteran, you moron, don't you know what day it is?! If he wants to stand in the middle of the road, let him. We can wait!"

Archie nods at the driver who almost hit him, who's now shouting at the driver behind him mashing his car horn in one long angry blast, to let him know he's thankful for his patience, and bolts, shaking off the memories.

Archie doesn't want to remember.

Archie's booted feet hit the Distillery District's cobblestones, and he barely notices the change from flat concrete to the uneven ground of rain-marooned bricks. He's not sure where he's headed; he's letting his boots lead him on. There isn't anyone here. The District's lanes and streets are empty as people have found shelter inside its many stores and coffee shops. Walking on the cobblestoned streets is like entering the past; Archie slows down, letting the unhurried pace of this empty place bind him into its timelessness.

Archie emerges from the long wide lane fenced in by the old distillery buildings into the cobblestoned street that cuts the district in half along the north-south axis. Archie hesitates as the sky lightens, and the rain peters into drizzle. He slides his hands out of his pockets and stands at ease, scanning the area, scrutinizing the odd person hurrying from one building to another or out to Mill Street, arms bent at right angles, coffee cups in their hands. He shakes his head at the superficiality of busyness. Archie feels like an alien, a person who can never be that coffee-cup holder, who can't afford the daily $6 latte or the normalcy of carrying a cup of coffee without fear of it being smacked out of his hand because he wasn't paying attention.

Archie draws his brows together and strides forward in hidden rage. He whips his legs one-two, one-two north along this pedestrian-only street then east along the cobblestoned lane toward Cherry Street. He hits its concrete sidewalk at almost a run, swerves right, and arrives at Lakeshore Boulevard in under five minutes. He jogs through the multi-laned traffic zipping underneath the concrete underside of the Gardiner Expressway and enters a ragged, neglected area west of Cherry filled with weeds and screed that he'd discovered a few months earlier. Archie hastens towards its water's industrial edge. Finally, he's there.

Archie's right hand strays underneath his jacket towards his Sig's grip.

I can't shoot here.

Archie remembers another spot, far away from anyone or any place where he practices on targets of old, fallen trunks of trees. But not here where there are lake freighters at docks and tug boats could appear—and the port with its police and customs officers who could recognize the sound of his pistol.

Archie aches to shoot.

But he cannot.

Archie had promised Andrew. And a man keeps his word. What kind of man would he be if he broke his promise? Resentment soaks Archie's heart in bile at Andrew once again extracting from him a promise to meet him, and worst of all, today, to meet him at the Cenotaph where he must remember, where people will spot his dress uniform pants, his military jacket, his poppy—

Archie searches inside his upper left-hand jacket pocket for the poppy Andrew had insisted that he must pin on and adjured him not to lose. *Yes, the poppy's still there*, he reassures himself. Its pin pricks him sharply; Archie retrieves his injured finger hastily. He doesn't suck on it, for the pain has left his mind.

Archie stands at attention. The familiar stance brings comfort into his soul. His eyes rove the industrial area with its wind-roughened water slapping against the rust-red hull of the docked lake freighter; the Toronto Islands with its far-off trees being stripped of their leaves; and, across the harbour from the Islands, the soaring glass and gold buildings of Toronto's financial district, impervious to wind and rain, punctuated by the sky-thrusting spire of the CN Tower. Archie empties his mind, but memories sneak in. Words and sounds, sensations of heat from oil and metal on fire and of the cold of a desert night, of his mother's wail when she'd called him on his flip phone and he'd inadvertently blurted out to her: "He's dead."

Archie shifts his feet. His vision fills with blood and brains, a blasted-off leg lying across vehicle debris, powdered with Afghanistan dust. The flashback suffocates his chest. He hyperventilates, struggling against his brain cycling air in and out rapidly, gasping for rescue, to replace the remembered sweet-sourness of blood and death with the freshness of wind-stormed water. A lake freighter's baritone horn resounds off his chest, blasting away the waves of memory. Archie blinks rapidly and refocuses on the reality before him of grey clouds upon grey clouds, of iron-grey water huffing up and down near his feet, of the grey concrete that lines the channel he's standing near...

Relief.

Archie feels nothing. And that's how Archie prefers living his story, hidden from even himself.

0959 HOURS

Chapter
10

Archie walks north, away from the Great Lake, past people walking toward him with poppies shining red in the rain. Poppies. Row upon row, coming at him, like nagging maids telling him to remember. Remember. Remember.

Remember.

Archie's mouth relaxes in a straight line, his deep brown-almost-black eyes look straight ahead, his cheeks unlined, his jaw set firmly, his arms swinging in the natural military rhythm in step with his feet. They obscure his seething thoughts, his screaming heart, and his soul pounding the dark, destructed walls of his innocence.

Archie's jaw jams teeth against teeth.

But the screaming continues.

Remember. Remember, say the poppies dancing past. One by one, row upon row.

Archie's body rebels at the popular command.

Archie almost releases control over his mouth to scream: "Stop!"

"Stop telling me to remember!"

Archie reaches an intersection, steps around the sharp corner of a stone building, and falls against its wall on the side street. He closes his eyes as Torontonians hurry past towards Queen and Bay, towards the Cenotaph and Remembrance Day. Bile rises as a voice emerges from the past to ring in his ears.

"Son, you need to man up," rebukes his father, whom he's called Sir for as long as he can remember. He and his twin Stephen call him Sir as a mark of outward obedience in Archie's mouth, flattering respect in Stephen's.

Archie had just told him over the flip-phone…

No, he admits to himself, he'd screamed: "Sir! Sir! Come—," and then his breath had failed him. His father had predictably repeated to man up and speak up. Archie cannot stop staring at Pawpaw, who is lying there at his feet, his faithful companion still in his hand flung out to the side. Pawpaw's head—

No! Archie drives his upper eyelids into his lower until his eyeballs object; he screams internally but out loud too apparently, for his father yells at him down the phone line: "Stop! Stop your screaming, boy. You're eighteen. You're an army man now. I won't have my son disgrace my name. Get it together."

Archie swallows hard. "It's…It's."

"Spit it out," Sir spits into his ear impatiently.

Archie lets out all his air and says: "It's Pawpaw." He swallows at the birthday cake that burns his throat, demanding ejection, to leave this horrible place of—

Archie's eyes have somehow opened themselves again, and he's staring at bits of grey and flecks of white, covered in gobs of blood.

"What about him?" his father asks, harshness roughing his voice.

"He's dead."

"He was alive when I left him. What did you do?"

"Nothing," Archie squeals. "Nothing!" he repeats, his voice pitching higher as his heart wonders why he'd done nothing. *Why did I sit there listening to Pawpaw and not seen nor heard the plans in his voice?*

I heard! Archie catches the sob at his silent admission. He hadn't believed it. Pawpaw had told him in the way he'd resisted his efforts to accept the tablet computer Archie had bought him. Archie had stopped in at the mega electronics store right after enlisting to buy one—his first thought on the way to Pawpaw's place being he and Pawpaw would need a way to talk directly without Sir's interference. His grandfather's home, the place where he felt he belonged the most, was the first place he wanted to go to after enlisting. "Here," he'd said, handing the tablet computer to his grandfather. And Pawpaw had said, "No son, you best have it. It'll serve you as you go off on your grand adventure. I had my own grand adventure. It's your turn. I can't go with you." The look in his eyes—

Archie sobs, and Sir hears him.

"What did you do, Archie? Tell me. And I'll make it right like I always do."

"Nothing, Sir. I did nothing. We all did nothing. Nothing can make this right. Pawpaw's dead." And then Archie flips the phone shut, turns it off, and squats down to stare at Pawpaw's half-blown-off head searching for his eyes, wondering if the sadness he'd seen in them, the finality of endurance, is still there. But the blood and bits of brain blown out by Pawpaw's gun covers everything.

"Grab his leg, Private! Now! Maybe those medics can get it the fucking back on him!"

Archie looks disbelievingly at his corporal. What do you mean, get it back on? Archie scans the scarred, tanned landscape with its stains of blood and holes of explosions. There is no leg.

"Private, I gave you an order. Do it now!"

Archie jumps at the ferocity in his corporal's voice. He stands to attention, salutes, and walks towards what he thinks is a leg. It's long; it has a bend in the middle; it's festooned with ribbons of desert camouflage with spatters of crimson, maroon, and red-black clots all over it. Bone chips litter the surrounding ground. Archie leans down to grab it with his black-gloved hand and halts. His lunch rises into his esophagus and demands release from this field of horrors. The corporal bangs into him from behind, thrusts him out of the way to grab the leg. Anger wrenches Archie, anger at the Taliban, at the primitive people who brought him to this place, anger at them blowing up the innocents in those buildings. *I was a kid. I didn't know about Taliban tactics.* Archie remembers how the news, his neighbours, shows, and posters had made war exciting, justice-making, a way out from his drab life into the grand adventure Pawpaw had told him life had held for him, to become a man's man.

Here he is, a man, a man leaning down to retrieve a shattered leg from his corporal who is trying to reattach it to his dead friend. Dust coats his nostrils; gore drying under the sun impregnates his memory. Urine and shit and blood commingle into death's sewage.

A sob heaves itself into his throat along with his lunch, and Archie pukes all over the blood-encrusted leg. Salt water streams down his face into his mouth; the salt is saltier than the crackers he used to crumble into his soup on Sunday lunches out after church. Church.

There are no churches here, only insignificant prayer services to a God who watches impassively overhead in this oven as humans run around killing each other. *My friend is dead. He leads services to you, God. Lead the services. Past tense. He's no more. He'll never lead anyone ever again.*

"Private! Give me that leg, now!"

Archie can't do it, he can't indulge his superior's fantasy. The reality facing him is too—

Over the din of a landing helicopter, his ears capture the blown-away words of the officer, the Lieutenant who's so young, his beard is fuzz. "He's dead. The leg doesn't matter. Leave your Private alone."

Archie glances over. The officer has his hand on the corporal's upper back, and the corporal's face is puce with rage. Under Archie's fear-stained eyes, the corporal's face transforms, it falls, it dissolves. Suddenly, the man is sobbing on his commanding officer's shoulder.

Men. We're men, here Sir, he thinks. *Real men. But not the kind you are; I'll never be a man to you, Sir.*

Archie lifts himself upright with his abdominal muscles, straining under the weight of his gear, which suddenly feels like lead. And walks back to where his friend lies in pieces. One leg gone, the other bent at a strange angle, his torso missing chunks like a malignant shark had attacked in a frenzy, and his face—his face. Archie swallows hard. He squats next to his friend, closes his eyes, drops his head, and recites the now-familiar prayer for the dead. And then he repeats the words his friend always begins their prayer meetings with. Began. Past tense. Dead tense. Tears drip off his chin to mingle with his friend's dead blood; then Archie opens his eyes, takes in one last gory look of respect, stands up, blinks the tears away, and walks over to help the medics identify and retrieve the latest bodies Taliban IEDs had created.

The imposing man has a face like leather; dark blue, dirty fabric encircles his head. Round and round, the fabric is wound, like an artistic hat. A strand hangs down at the side, down to his shoulder. The man is Afghani. Archie imagines he's the man who blew up his friend. The man who armed and buried the IED to explode apart another man he would never know, didn't care to know. We are not humans to them. Archie is standing impassively as the Canadians speak friendly like to this man. It's his first tour of duty as an American seconded to the Canadians. He thinks of himself as embedded, a stealth American, hidden from the Taliban and Americans both, surveying them from safety. But how safe? It's his first patrol with the Canadians, and they're in a village to search out Taliban. Archie hates the Canadians' relaxed body language, their friendliness with these people, these people whose sole purpose is to shoot up and explode apart his friends, these people who started it all by blowing up Americans going about their business, the same Americans who keep these people's fucking heroin economy afloat.

Archie stands impassively, his arms relaxed on his machine gun, his legs apart in an easy but ready stance, his boots firmly planted on the ground, but inside them, his toes are like springs ready to pounce, ready to pound that man's face into pulp at the slightest twitch. Rage bubbles and froths inside Archie like a cauldron that doesn't have an off switch, whose contents boil into steam that never exhaust themselves dry.

His new Sergeant Nadine shifts her stance slightly so that she's abruptly closer to him. Her calm energy radiates into him; her body heat seems to reach through the country's heat sweating him inside his camouflage and underneath his gear, to soothe him. Nadine says nothing...

...but he's relaxing against the stone wall, and its November-chill is seeping through his outer jacket, his dress uniform jacket, and his crisp shirt. The dry cleaning's ethereous fumes have faded. The light is dim; the rain has diminished to drops that hit his face sporadically, its clean taste a contrast to the salt staining the corners of his mouth. Archie pulls the brim of his Tilley hat down until all he can see is the rain-blackened concrete sidewalk underneath his spattered boots and the road's run-off flowing along the gutter beside it.

A poppy slides into view in the gutter; the rain water gushing toward the drain takes the dead red plastic along with it. The poppy spills through the bars on its watery ride and disappears. Archie clamps his teeth against the grief that threatens to engulf him, to drown him into hours of crying. Every night but last night has been torments of tears, and he's sick of them. He's sick of crying endlessly. It never stops, clogging his nose, swelling his eyes, itching his face, filling his throat, and coating his tongue with bits of snot, while the wound in his heart pulses on. Never, ever stops. At best, the traumatic wound only retreats into his subconscious waiting for a poppy, a word, a look, a day of remembrance to come along and kick it, flare the pain up in his dying, broken heart again. *When will it stop? Why won't it stop? Why is it immortal when my friend was mortal? Why is isolation the only safe response to it?* Archie blinks away more memories trying to crawl into his head, making their past his present again, memories of the last words of Sally, his father, the silence of his mother, as they informed him how he was killing their peace he'd fought for, how he needed to—

No! He yells internally. *No, no, no!*

Their suffering had ended when he'd left them. His suffering remains with him always. Crying and anger, his two faithful companions, along with Pawpaw's Outdoorsman that had obeyed his grandfather's final command to blow his brains through his skull all over his polished wooden floor.

Pawpaw had cleaned his house from the small attic at the top of the house to the dusty basement at the bottom. He'd bleached his basement walls and the counters of his kitchen. Pawpaw had hoovered his decades-old sofa and chairs in the living room until the pile was almost like new. He'd dusted every surface and polished every piece of furniture. Pawpaw had polished the wood floors of the first and second stories until the sheen had reflected Archie and Sir as they'd stared at Pawpaw's body and later the paramedics who'd confirmed Pawpaw had left this earth a shattered mess. Chlorine smell had conflicted with the lemon scent of floor polish. As he'd drunk in the shining clean of Pawpaw's home, Archie had thought how he'd acquiesced to Pawpaw's unusual insistence that he stay seated on his usual worn porch chair and not help him bring out the bottles of beer, chips, and birthday cake slices to share companionably. Beer and chips on the porch had been their ritual: the arguing over which beer was better. Pawpaw always offered him Molson's. Archie always insisted on Labatt's. They'd bicker, and Pawpaw would stare at him with those glacial-blue eyes, saying, he had no good taste while handing him the Labatt's and telling him he knew where the chips were, to go get them, and to not leave them in a bag but put them in a bowl. "We're not pigs here," he'd lecture him.

The fridge was empty; the cupboards were bare. Archie only discovered that after finding Pawpaw dead.

Pawpaw had brought him his Labatt's and had talked about the new tablet computer and Archie's grand adventure in words that meant he wasn't going to be here, but Archie hadn't heard the message, only the words.

A spill of water from an eavestrough overhead splashes onto Archie's Tilley hat and shocks him back to the present, to the cold November Remembrance Day.

Archie shakes himself. The memories had almost dragged him into the worst day, the absolute worst day.

Archie pushes himself off the wall and starts walking. He strains to focus on the material world. The poppies, some half-falling off as their pins let go of their spot on Torontonians' shiny jackets, come at him row upon row. Andrew's meandering line of poppies up his right arm thrusts itself into his internal view. Archie flinches. He doesn't want to remember. He doesn't want to know. Archie speeds up, his strides lengthening, taking him further and further away from the Cenotaph and his duty there.

Mercifully, the memories stop their march into his consciousness. The worst one halts in its rise out of the depths as his booted feet pound down the sidewalk faster and faster.

"You're alone."

"You don't belong."

"You need to get over it."

"You're back here now. Time to get a job."

"You're not injured. You got your legs, your arms. Those men, over there," Sir says, pointing an arthritic finger, with its knobs of joints and skeletal pieces, at the veterans nearby in their wheelchairs. "Those men," he scolds Archie, "are real men who made real sacrifices." He'd turned on his heel and marched out, flinging at him over his shoulder: "I'm ashamed of you. No son of mine is a malingerer. Your brother has made a man of himself. But what do you expect, he's the older twin."

Archie hadn't heard his last words. His VA counsellor had come into the waiting room then, seeking the person who's supposed to be with Archie. Archie had had to tell him that his father had left; Archie's mouth clamps shut against repeating his father's words. But his counsellor knows; he's seen their mark in Archie's deep brown eyes. Archie recognizes his counsellor's understanding in the softening around his cheeks and mouth, in the gentle hand that comforts his shoulder and steers him towards his plain office.

Someone grabs Archie's arm, and he whips around, his hand cocked and stops his movement as he sees the rain-spattered face of an older woman with her fading blue eyes wide. Archie drops his arm and his hand. "I'm sorry, ma'am."

She shakes her head. "It's okay, You were about to walk into the path of that truck," she points down the road toward a fast-disappearing white courier truck, its red taillights like two accusatory orbs.

"Thank you, ma'am," Archie says quietly, thinking it's too bad she'd grabbed his arm and saved his physical body. Archie doesn't know where his soul is hiding, yet it feels trapped in this place, in this life. Archie stands at attention on the edge of the curb, his hands clasped behind his back, his feet apart. His soul wants out of this hellhole. The war continues in his head; Archie's heart burns from the poison of people's hatred and condemnation.

I will never recover.

Death is the only recovery.

The light turns green. The woman tells him as she steps off the curb, "Thank you for your service, young man. You are a hero."

Archie remains frozen in place. If only she knew his real thoughts.

<u>1030 HOURS</u>

Chapter

11

Ｔᴇɴ-ᴛʜɪʀᴛʏ ʜᴏᴜʀs. Aʀᴄʜɪᴇ approaches Queen and Bay. The strains of World War Two music piped through speakers waft towards his ears. Mournful and nostalgic. From a time even before Pawpaw, who used to tell him tales of his father raising extra cattle to feed the soldiers overseas. "Farming sinewed arms and strained backs," Pawpaw had related, rocking in his chair on his porch, his Outdoorsman in his calloused, knobbed hands. "It was hard work and an honour for the country. Now, it's just hard, and no one gives a damn," he'd spat. Archie had nodded, not really comprehending but figuring Pawpaw knew these things.

Archie slows down to a walk then a stroll. His arms stop swinging, and his hands hang loose by his sides. The window shopper up ahead pauses, and he joins her at the window. Archie stares at the fancy dresses that he can't imagine any woman he knows wearing while his senses follow the people moving behind him, around him, their pace, their direction, their energy signals. Many hurry, serious in their busyness; some stroll arm in arm; and a few gossip, their shoes clicking along with their tongues like chickens pecking. Archie turns his head slightly to the left, to survey where he must go. The crowds are gathering at the angled intersection of Queen and Bay; he watches the backs of trench-coated people walking ponderously toward it, while men in suits weave through the crowd on their way to appointments and mediations.

The table is long and oblong. Men sit on one side; Archie sits opposite them.

Archie shakes his head. *I'm not going there. Breathe!* Archie inhales, holds city air deep in the alveoli of his lungs, and releases it gradually into the damp. Archie turns on his heel and marches south down Bay. He turns left at the first intersection and marches east along Richmond Street. He turns left on Yonge and marches north to Queen. He halts. And watches.

The music reaches him faintly here, as he's not quite at the level of the Queen Street sidewalk. Archie steps sideways into the alcove that leads to stairs down to the subway and below-level shopping. People are walking one by one, two by two like ragged streamers towards the Cenotaph. Archie pokes his head around the corner. In the distance, the front of a fire truck faces him. Men in their bulky tan fire suits with their thick fluorescent-yellow lines cross-hatched on their backs, stand around near the back of it. Men in dark uniforms—blue or black he cannot tell from this distance in the grey-dim light—mingle with them. A man pushing a stroller with his black backpack sagging down his back follows a woman wearing a long wool black coat, black pants, her blonde hair ruffling in the wind; a cyclist wheels his bike across the street. Archie narrows his eyes. Cyclists don't walk their bikes in this town. What is he up to? The cyclist's black helmet sits down low on his forehead, and wrap-around shades hide his eyes. A knapsack hugs his back. Archie follows him with his eyes as he wheels his bike past the firefighters and the first responders in their dress uniforms. The emergency professionals don't notice the cyclist. Archie shakes his head internally at their casual indifference to the potential dangers around them.

Archie's eyes widen. They shift back and forth, scanning Queen Street near the fire truck. He's lost the cyclist. Archie curses his inattention. *How did I let civilians distract me? Their lax training is no excuse, Specialist. Stay on task, Specialist!*

"Pay attention, Private! We're not girls here!"

"Yes, sir!" Archie replies, snapping his feet together and saluting.

"Fifty push-ups now!"

Archie drops to the ground, flattens his hands, and grunts as he pushes against the concrete to lift his body weight. "On your fingers, Private!" Archie had learnt the hard way not to stop the continual motion of raising and lowering his plank-like body while shifting from hands flat on the ground to the tips of his fingers. A grunt was the only sign of satisfaction, resentful satisfaction Archie had grinned to himself, that he had made it.

A woman brushes the sleeve of his jacket, and Archie jumps back, his legs tense, his right hand under his jacket grabbing his Sig's grip. Archie forces himself to let go as he watches her walk swaying across Queen at an angle toward and in front of the Eaton Centre entrance. The woman's making a zig-zagging beeline to the hefty female vet handing out poppies from her white box slung around her neck and resting on her ample chest. The vet looks old enough to have been in the Viet Nam war. Archie salutes her courage silently. Those were the last fifty extra I had to do in basic training. No one's caught me out in inattention since then, not during training, not during battle. It shouldn't have happened now.

"Got you!"

Archie jumps, his hand cocked and flying toward the familiar voice of Nadine's ex. Archie thrusts up an arm but stops himself short. They're eye to bloodshot eye. Archie sizes him up. Nadine's ex is sleep deprived and hungover. His hair is uncombed, and his jacket is half up on one shoulder to his neck, half off the other shoulder, and unzipped. The wind flaps his creased checked shirt underneath. His rumpled pants hang low, their hems dragging on the ground. *That'll trip him up*, Archie assesses. Outwardly, he relaxes his body. Inwardly, Archie turns his feet in their hard boots into springs while his hands hang by his side, relaxed and open, ready to grab his combat pistol.

Nadine's ex sways and points a finger into Archie's chest: "You. Are. Having. An. Affair. With. My. Girlfriend."

"She's not your girlfriend any longer," Archie replies in that friendly voice the Canadian military had taught him.

The ex stares at him with bleary eyes: "She is. She just doesn't know it."

"Nadine knows her own mind."

"She's just mad at me. She'll get over it."

"Why?"

"Why?" the ex's eyes widen, revealing their whites ribboned with red. "Why!" he shouts.

Archie grabs his left arm with his right hand, pulls him toward him, whips him around, making the man stagger and fall against his chest, his left arm painfully wrenched up high on his back but out of sight of passersby. Archie marches him across Yonge Street, down south, then left onto Richmond, which is empty of pedestrians, and shoves him up against the red stone wall of the grand building that borders the sidewalk.

Archie states: "She won't get over it. I visited her in hospital. Why would she go to you for more beatings?"

The ex opens his mouth like a fish, gulps twice, and squeaks: "You're hurting me."

Archie's mouth grimaces in contempt. He wants to belt this man; hit his soft jaw with his hard fist, feel the solid jawbone give under his justice punch, see the blood squirt from his tongue as his teeth bite it in fear; feel the tremor of his legs as he kicks them out from underneath the man; watch him fall like a ragged, contemptible doll;

and hear the satisfactory smoosh of hair-cushioned skull on concrete.

Archie narrows his eyes until they're slits of black, he pulls his lips back into a snarl, and observes the blood leaving Nadine's ex's face as Archie envisions pushing the efficient muzzle of his Sig into the middle of the man's forehead and squeezing the trigger towards himself, watching the sure knowledge of what would happen next come into the eyes of this disgusting specimen of a human. The sudden paleness of this non-human pinned by Archie's raging strength bulges his eyes into protuberant rounds of whites trashed by fatigue and drink.

Archie pushes hard against him, forcing the man up and up against the wall until only his toes touch the ground. Sickly sweat punctures the chill. Archie releases him and strides away, his back to him, confident that the ex will not bother him again.

Nadine's ex doesn't follow.

Archie reaches Queen Street, his rage propelling him on to the Cenotaph and past it to the western edge of the Eaton Centre at Alexander. Archie halts. He scans his surroundings. A yellow fire hydrant stands guard to his right, monitoring the eastern end of the half-circle driveway that swoops in front of the entrance to Old City Hall. Television satellite trucks sit on either side of the street, one black, one white, both facing Queen Street with long steel poles sticking straight up out of their tops, fat steel wires swirling up them. Police in their light-sucking black uniforms stand around, some with hands in their pockets, the word "POLICE" in white on their backs. A man in a leather jacket carries a closed umbrella, head down. Women in silver puffy jackets and black puffy jackets with belts encircling their waists and long tan trench coats carry black purses and sport red poppies on their lapels as they walk towards the woman handing out white brochures. From his distant post, Archie narrows his eyes to read the glossy paper booklets the woman is whipping out faster than eyes can see as people come up to her, hands outstretched. *Programs*, he surmises.

Archie doesn't need one.

This is his second Remembrance Day—it's as seared into him as every Veterans Day his father had forced him to attend along with his twin, in honour of the men who'd served.

Run, his feet itch.

Stay, his brain commands.

Cry, his heart melts.

Rage, his stomach clenches.

The World War Two music stops.

It's 1045 hours.

The silence is eerie, like waiting for an explosion, knowing it's coming yet not knowing when.

Run!

In front of him, a knot of soldiers stand waiting in their green dress uniforms, not a crease to be seen across their broad shoulders and through their nipped-in waists or in the flaps that cover their butts. Their berets are cocked at the correct angle. The soldiers' controlled stillness shores up Archie's self-control.

Archie sidles down Alexander, past a man tucked in behind one of the enormous black pots that hold vertical palms and dangling flowers and fat cabbages, until he's far enough not to be in that man's space and to be alone in his own. The man is all in green and tan camouflage from his sagging, wet hat pulled low to his well-worn sneakers half hidden underneath his cotton-polyester pants. His blue backpack and red poppy are the only anomalies of colour on him.

Andrew's voice seeps into Archie's mind, urging him to cross the street and join the crowd on the northern side of the drive. Archie hadn't gone back to his room to retrieve the device, and the people surging in now from the Eaton Centre and the subway, the groups of adult students being instructed by their teachers on what this day is about and how it will go, the military men and women, the bicycle police in their fluorescent-yellow jackets, the young girls handing out poppies, the well-dressed business couple, the natty lawyer with his row of medals pinned on his striped blue suit, the children being pushed in their strollers, and the men wheeling themselves in their chrome and black wheelchairs—all coming towards him send up panic signals to his brain. Archie pants; his heart beats against his ribs; his fingers flex closed and open, closed and open as they try to fist and he tries to relax them.

The faint strains of horns and tubas and drums and flutes march towards him. A grey stealth police car drives slowly into his view, and the band appears behind it as it angles towards Queen from Bay while they march confidently in their black and red uniforms, tassels swinging, towards the semi-circular driveway and the dignitaries standing at the top of Old City Hall's steps. Behind them come the colours, the Canadian flag leading the Ontario, British, and military flags carried by men and women in their green dress uniforms with their wide white belts, yellow shoulder braids, and red berets.

Archie scoots.

Archie marches down Alexander to the back of Old City Hall. Once behind its protective hulk, Archie stops and turns, his lungs heaving for air as he listens to the service from far off, as far as he dares to go while still keeping his promise to Andrew. The music falls silent. A voice stirs the air. The movement of people stills. The silence stretches. Emptiness fills him. A bugle mourns.

Chills race up and down his body.

Archie resists trembling.

A drone above him vibrates the hushed air. Archie lifts his head and regards detached the Missing Man formation fly overhead. Archie's eyes stray to the Harvard trailing the three flying in front of it in a V-formation. The Missing Man, the Lost Man. The man who doesn't come back. The man at peace, eternally. Archie follows the

Lost Man with his eyes until that plane disappears over the height of
the buildings to his east.

1100 HOURS

Chapter

12

THE BUGLE SIGNALS the start of two minutes of silence. The city hushes around Archie. Then it's over, and the noise of daily life resumes as the crowd disperses. Archie knows he's to meet Andrew and the others, yet his heart contracting in pain resists. He feels better in Andrew's company; he feels less alone when with the others. Their energies lighten him, pull him into life, and willingly he submits. Yet his heart wants to fold inwards, curl up like a fetus, warm and safe in its sac of ribs. People are dangerous, his heart lies to him. And he hears it as truth. Andrew is both a safe place to be and dangerous; always Archie must war against the lie taking hold. Most of the time he loses that war, but today he yearns to obey Andrew's command no matter how much his heart squeezes into itself until pain shards strike paths throughout his muscles and joints.

Archie shifts slightly at his post behind Old City Hall.

Archie arrests himself. He stands erect, his eyes scanning the faces, the movements, the sounds, the smells of returning cars as they roar out their exhaust. He can't seem to move; his boots, like glue, fasten him to the wet sidewalk. Two men in green dress uniforms of RCR march toward him. He wants to say something, to show respect to members of the Royal Canadian Regiment, the oldest regular force infantry regiment in Canada. But he cannot. One of them sidles his eyes towards him as they stride past. The man stops, and his companion slows and turns around to stand next to him.

"Hello soldier," the first one says. "May I help you?"

Archie is stunned. He spots the rank on the man's right sleeve and unconsciously straightens his upper back and neck. Archie says: "I'm looking for my old commanding officer, sir."

"At ease, soldier." The officer hesitates, searching for signs of rank or what brigade Archie belongs to, but Archie had put no identifying patches on his outer jacket sleeves that morning. He'd taken them off his dress uniform the day he left New Mexico. "Which regiment?"

Archie tells him. The officer nods and tells Archie he saw Andrew and two other people with him on the other side of Old City Hall. He leans forward and points around the back northeast corner of the old pink-stone building. Archie follows his finger, and his feet release themselves from the wet and begin moving toward Bay Street and Alexander.

Archie flows with others on the narrow sidewalk, holding himself in check, his self-control reset by the encounter. Poppies on jackets glow red in the resuming rain. The plastic flowers' centres are like black holes. Some half dangle on their precarious pins; some are embedded, their pins weaving in and out, in and out of their wool-coat homes. Eleven o'clock is done; poppies are meant to be off. Fury flares into Archie's breast, and so when he spots Nadine's ex hunting around, swerving between people, his face turning this way and that, his eyes searching every person he passes—for him? No, Nadine!—Archie lengthens his stride, puffs out his chest, sucks in his stomach, and swings his arms straight, propelling himself right at the ex. Archie lifts his right arm and holds it ahead of him in one of its forward-momentum swings as he approaches from behind. Archie grabs the back of the ex's collar and thrusts it up, lifting the man up onto his tippy toes. He allows his momentum to keep him going and to propel the ex ahead of him. He executes a sharp right turn as he stretches his right arm upward, raising the man so that his toes leave the asphalt road long enough for him to turn with Archie ahead of him. The ex windmills his arms, trying to grab backward purchase on Archie. But Archie's arms are like trunks of iron; even at full extension, his longer arms are the stronger. Archie and Nadine's ex arrive at the north end of Nathan Phillips Square, where Archie drops the man. The ex's legs buckle, and he lands on his hands while Archie glares at him, his fingers curling and uncurling to extend fully out like two sets of five daggers. The man springs up and twists around, yelling: "Hey! Whatdya do that for?"

"You were stalking Nadine."

"I don't stalk."

"What were you doing?"

"I was looking for her. Is it a crime to look for her?"

"Yes."

The ex blinks; hidden blood swells its conduits and floods up his neck to his cheeks to disappear into his hairline. He shouts, spitting thick saliva at Archie's face: "No! It's not!"

Archie doesn't flinch. He assesses the chances of shooting him dead, solving Nadine's problem finally. Pistol. Death. The ultimate solution. Does he want to be caught? No, he answers himself. He's not ready yet. He hasn't found Andrew yet, and his mission is to meet up with Andrew, David, and Nadine, not to be detained or execute his inevitable release from himself.

Archie cocks his head and lowers his thick, black lashes to ponder the ex through them. The man involuntarily takes a step backwards and shrinks within himself. Perhaps shooting him would do him a favour: it will release Nadine's ex from his pain, too. Emotions are eating him up inside. The ex can't help himself; it seems like he needs to look for Nadine, look for reasons that she left him, reasons that have nothing to do with Archie but that keep him innocent, the one not responsible, the one not to blame for his misery. Perhaps shooting him quickly, taking the pistol out of its conceal carry in one swift action and pulling the trigger before he even has time to blink is the best option.

The ex is a dangerous man.

He can't help himself.

Perhaps he's mentally ill.

They say that the mentally ill would rather harm themselves than another.

This man wants to harm Nadine.

He is not mentally ill.

He's just bad.

And men turned dangerous by their emotions deserve to be shot, to preserve the good of society.

Nadine's ex has stopped breathing. His red-shot eyes bulge unblinking, glued to Archie's impassive face with their lowered lids and irises darkening to obsidian. Archie notes the man's fear, unconsciously shifts his weight forward, and lengthens his torso muscles, making his average-height frame seem to tower over Nadine's ex.

Archie sends his mind into his skin's receptors to perceive the energy in the air through his clothing. He senses people walking by, intent on their destinations, lost in their iPhones and Androids, busy talking to each other, none noticing him. He attunes his mind to the sounds his ears capture: fences scrape and scream against asphalt and concrete as workers remove them from their stations and pack them up. The workers, too, don't notice the two men frozen in their mental dance of prey and predator.

But as swift as Archie is—and he practiced on the battlefields of Afghanistan many times—saved his combat unit's lives one time because of his speed and accuracy—Archie knows that once the pistol explodes the bullet out its muzzle, blasting the sound barrier, it will alert all the ears around him. They will to a person notice, except the ones wearing earbuds or colossal headphones pumping isolating music into their heads. People will lift their heads and look around, querying gun shot or car backfiring? And they will spot him with a man dead on the ground at his feet.

Archie doesn't have a silencer.

Archie rues the error, the omission. But then he's not sure he could've fit a silencer at the end of his Sig inside his left-hand pants pocket.

Archie decides, and Nadine's ex comes to life. The ex turns on his heels and runs, weaving in and out between sets of twos and threes as the crowd surges north. Archie watches him go.

When the ex is lost to his view, Archie releases all the tension in his abdomen, legs, and arms with one command: Relax. Archie swivels on his heels. He walks casually south, scanning the crowd for the familiar faces of Andrew, David, and Nadine. The people coming towards him unconsciously change directions as they approach. Archie doesn't notice. *I should tell Andrew of the encounter*, Archie thinks. *Transparency is crucial to the smooth operation of a combat unit, even in civilian life. I owe Andrew that much.*

A SHOUT CAUSES Archie to whirl. He spots Andrew waving at him to come over towards the south end of the vast Nathan Phillips Square. Archie walks measuredly toward them; his heart burns to reverse course, to be alone in his pain. His feet slow. Andrew watches, and his eyes capture Archie's and pull him to them. David has his head down over his iPhone. Nadine has her iPhone out, too. Archie fights the pain and draws near. He halts in front of Andrew, clicks his feet, and salutes smartly. Andrew salutes back and tells him to be at ease. Suddenly, the pain seeps out of Archie's body like brakes releasing their pressure. He's glad he obeyed Andrew.

"David and Nadine are discussing where to have lunch," Andrew says, jerking his head toward the two. Archie shifts his eyes to look at them then back up at Andrew. Andrew is tall, filled out with muscle and flesh but not fat. Archie usually defers to his commanding officer, but the thought of lunch brings bile up into his throat. "If you don't mind, sir, I'd like to be excused."

"No," Andrew replies.

Nadine raises her head and regards the two men with guarded eyes.

Archie's eyes widen. Andrew normally lets him be. But not today. Archie shifts his feet closer to each other. "I'm not hungry, sir."

"You can have a drink while we eat, Archie."

"I'd rather not."

"Today is not a good day to be alone."

Archie's iPhone pings in his pocket. Archie slides it out and reads the message on the lock screen. "Nadine needs us all there."

Archie's mouth sours. He slides his right thumb across the message on the screen, quickly types in his passcode, and launches Signal. He replies: "I've seen her ex. Dispatched him. She doesn't need me there."

David doesn't lift his head from his iPhone as he reads Archie's message and replies. Andrew waits, watching David's thumbs typing in a blur. Nadine's eyes are darting here and there. Archie notices. His iPhone pings in his hand. He reads: "What happened?"

Archie types back: "Nothing."

Seconds later, another ping: "He's persistent. Nadine can't get rid of him. Why would you?"

"I have my weapon, and he knows it."

From David's almost-silent breath in, Archie knows when David has read his message. David lifts his head and scrutinizes his face.

Archie returns his look impassively. David darts his eyes towards Andrew then drops his head back to his iPhone. Andrew unlocks his iPhone and waits. Ever since they returned from Afghanistan, David has said not one word, has verbalized nothing but breath sounds. He can't even sigh heavily. Instead, he messages them all through Signal. Not email, not regular text messaging, not through social media, but Signal only. Signal's name is a flag to his muteness; its privacy and security a revolt against constant attack. The three of them accepted his voice shutting down. As long as he still talks to them, in whatever manner makes him comfortable, is good with them. Andrew and David finish their conversation. Andrew turns back to Archie: "You're joining us. It's unanimous."

Nadine states: "The women in Afghanistan were only free behind doors, under ceilings, inside their walls. There, they joined each other. Not alone."

The three men slowly turn their heads to blink confusedly at her. Nadine fixes her gaze on the sky overhead laden with clouds' tears. She says: "They saw us the same as their oppressors. Men arbitrarily killing their men, bombing their homes. One of them told me this on my fourth visit to her home as she served me tea. It was so murky in there, except for her dress." Nadine lowers her eyes to the men's height and meets their astonished gaze.

Andrew tells her: "We went to save the women and girls. We gave them the freedom to access education. We weren't their oppressors."

Archie isn't sure what to think. Nadine has always been straightforward, not prone to embellishment. And Andrew's Canadian platoon was nothing like his American one.

Nadine replies: "That's what she told me, sir. She showed me photos of her male relatives, all dead from our allies. They were creased from how often she stared at them. She missed them, and all she had left were their photos."

"The Taliban were their oppressors."

"She said you are all the same. She said what difference did we make, except we allied ourselves with the ones who beat us and stole from us, I mean, them."

Andrew compresses his lips. Archie holds his breath as he glances at Nadine then back to Andrew. David stands stock still. Andrew says: "Alright, I concede there were some irregularities. But we were there to save them from the Taliban. We worked with the locals to bring education to the women and girls. We liberated them from oppressive dress codes. We sat in circles with the men to be accepted by each local community. Women no longer had to worry about being whipped because their ankles showed! You were there, Nadine. I concede being a woman you had a privilege the rest of us didn't have. But our intentions were good."

"They wanted us to leave."

"We did." Andrew's clipped voice leaves no room for dissent. "We went to help them, Sergeant, and we did that while we could."

Nadine's features fall into impassivity. Her spine stiffens, and she clasps her iPhone with both hands behind her back. Nadine shifts her booted feet into the at-ease position. Apart but rigidly holding her erect.

Andrew repeats: "We went to help them, Sergeant. We listened. We helped. They weren't alone in their struggle."

"Yes sir," Nadine replies.

Archie shoots his eyes towards Nadine, who returns his stare with an empty one of her own. Archie's heart flips. His conscious mind rejects what he sees. Archie blurts: "Okay."

Puzzlement draws Andrew's eyebrows up as he shifts his gaze to Archie. "Okay what?"

"Okay, I'll join you, sir. For lunch."

Andrew relaxes his shoulders and smiles at Archie. "Good!" he exclaims as he claps Archie on his upper back and clasps his shoulder before letting go. Andrew gestures with his iPhone, and the four gather in a four-sided circle, facing each other, heads down over their respective iPhones, to argue silently through group messaging where to go.

The four pick Fran's on College.

1230 HOURS

Chapter 13

Forks clink against plates, glasses rattle in the background, muffled shouts stream through the swinging kitchen door. Every time Fran's front glass door opens, sounds of cars splashing through driving rain join the homey cacophony. Archie, Andrew, David, and Nadine hustle in moments before the rain begins again. The four flap the few drops from their collars and Archie his Tilley hat. Enticing scents greet them—bacon sizzling out of sight, tabletop jugs of maple syrup sugaring the warm air, butter releasing comforting aromas as it melts on pancakes, tomatoes wafting warmth of soups, sweet apple pie steaming its come-eat-me scents—each veteran half-close their eyes to inhale the essences of their favourite food. Shoulders drop; smiles appear.

The hostess spots them standing halfway back in the queue. She shoos the people in front of them aside, who gladly give way. "Let these men and woman through," she instructs. "They've served for our freedom. The least we can do is let them through and sit them down to ease their tired legs." The queue shuffles to the side, leaving a clear path between the four and her. "That's it," she approves, nodding her neatly coiffed head with its smooth French bun. "So much marching, huh?" she addresses them.

Andrew barely got a "Yes, ma'am" out before she continued.

"You are all so brave. I can't believe you'd go over there to serve in that hellhole. Come this way. Follow me. Yes, you deserve to rest your legs. I have a nice booth for the four of you. You slide in there, young man, young lady, you slide in that one opposite. The men here can wait for you two to sit first. That's it. Here are your menus. You have a nice lunch now. I'll bring you coffee on the house."

The whirlwind left, and Andrew and David stare after her while Nadine settles herself opposite Archie. *What do I do with my jacket?* Archie wonders. He spots the chrome pole attached to the booth with four pegs. He slides out of his seat, removes his jacket, doffs his Tilley hat, and hangs them up on one peg. He slides back in. Andrew and David follow, Andrew sitting next to Archie, David next to Nadine.

The four interlace their chilled fingers, resting them on the table-covering menus shrunk-wrapped in plastic, as they drop their heads to stare at the long list of food items. Nadine slips her hands off the table and sits back, wrapping her arms around her waist.

"Right, men, let's eat. What are you having?" Andrew booms, sitting back as he picks up his menu. He looks over at Nadine: "Nadine, you must be hungry, too?"

David nudges her with his elbow. Nadine glances at him. He nods at her menu. She shakes her head. He glares at her, widening his eyes till the whites almost pop out, and pulling his bottom lip down until it curls over to reveal his small white even bottom teeth. She laughs, releases herself from her hug, and picks her menu up. David rearranges his face back to normal.

"Archie?" Andrew half-asks, half-commands.

Archie tears his eyes away from the opposite tableau and unclasps his hands to pick up the menu. The four disappear behind their laminated menus. They don't move, except for Andrew, who straightens his elbows to see his menu better. "The usual?" he asks.

The other three are mum.

David reaches into his dress jacket's inner uniform pocket and pulls out his iPhone, re-buttoning up his jacket with one hand after he lays his iPhone down on the clean table. Andrew lowers his menu and lays his smartphone on the table. Nadine and Archie echo his movements. David shakes his head at Andrew and flaps his menu up, glancing over at Nadine's stock-still face hidden from the other two by the menu she is holding up high again. David glances over at Andrew, who nods imperceptibly.

"Alright," Andrew says, lowering his parade volume. "We'll choose different today. The remembrance is over; now we eat. And we'll eat well. We feast for ourselves and for our lives, the ones we're living for our—"

"Here you go," their waitress says as she clatters a tray down on the table and lifts off one at a time white, thick-walled cups of coffee filled to the brim and plunks them down in front of each of them, sloshing coffee into their saucers, the hot bitterness fragrancing their table. Archie smiles to himself and steals a glimpse at Andrew's face. Andrew's face is wooden. Oblivious to Andrew's disapprobation of her messiness, the waitress beams at them, picks up her tray, tucks it under her arm to pull out her paper order pad and a pencil, and chirps: "May I take your order?" She tucks a stray lock of blonde-brown hair behind her ear; the lock falls out and swings in front of her left eye again.

Archie's lips twitch as Andrew's back straightens into an iron rod. Andrew folds his hands over each other carefully. "We're not ready," Andrew informs her, his clipped tones flying over the waitress's head. She pips: "No problem. I'll be back in five minutes." The waitress turns on her cushioned heel and walks over to the next table where three men sit, one crooking his finger at her. Archie watches her back as she talks to the man with the crooked finger. Her back tightens as the man leans forward, his fingers on the table edging closer and closer imperceptibly to where she's standing. The waitress laughs too brightly and shifts her weight away from him, placing her hand on her hip closest to him, taking the tray out from under her arm and letting it swing carelessly in front of her. The customer frowns and leans back. He waves her away. The waitress nods and hurries into the kitchen, tray thrust up under her arm.

Sensing action, Nadine peeks around her menu. "Who're you watching, Archie?" Nadine asks.

Archie jerks his head over to the swinging kitchen door. "The waitress."

"Oh. Do you know what you're having?"

"No."

"What about you, Nadine?" Andrew asks her.

"I'm not sure."

Nadine's small tone, her unsureness, bother Archie. She's usually the one who leads, who tells them what they want to eat. Archie blurts: "Remember my first day with your platoon?"

"I do!" Andrew booms.

Archie keeps his eyes on Nadine. "Remember that breakfast you served?"

Nadine shakes her head.

"Aw c'mon Nadine, you remember? You served me maple syrup! You poured it all over my eggs and then made me eat them. I thought my tongue was gonna shrivel up and die under sweetness onslaught. We know how to make good pie, but man you got us all beat in sweet things." Archie shakes his head and chuckles.

Nadine smiles.

Andrew grins. "Your face, Archie! It was priceless. I thought Nadine had fed you poison."

"It was, sir."

"Maple syrup is not poison!" Nadine retorts, a little of her old volume back in her voice.

Archie pours it on: "It was poison. It rotted my teeth. You didn't tell me y'all have dentures. Americans know how to keep our teeth. See!" Archie bares his teeth, revealing even white incisors, his front teeth two lines of bright fences. Nadine bares hers back, showing teeth more even and white than his. "I got you beat, Specialist."

"Ha!" Archie says. David muffles a laugh.

Andrew drawls: "We all got the Brits beat."

Guffaws erupt from Nadine and Archie. Menus lower to the table as Archie chokes out: "Remember that one guy? What was his name? Doesn't matter. Remember how he was eating your syrupy eggs Nadine, and a tooth falls out. What's this crunchy thing, he goes. And David there, David—," Archie convulses, laughter cutting off his air supply. Nadine clutches her stomach and gasps out: "David said, 'It's your tooth, sir.'"

Andrew hoots, slapping the table and rearing back against the booth's vinyl-covered cushioned back. David shakes silently, his eyes dancing, his lips curving up.

"He looked at David like he'd spoken Swahili, rolled his tongue around, spits that brown tooth out into his hand, and says, I believe you're right."

The four fall against the table, eyes half-shut, hands clutching stomachs, mouths wide in remembered jest. Nadine jostles her cup of coffee, spilling some of it into her saucer and onto the table. Archie sobers suddenly, grabs a bunch of napkins from the napkin dispenser at his end of the booth, and wipes the coffee up before Andrew goes all rigid on them. He knows Andrew won't chastise Nadine, but Andrew's thing is neatness. And today, they're all taking care of each other.

The laughter dies down, and the menus rise back up.

Archie declares: "I'm not having eggs."

Nadine chokes on a laugh from behind her menu. She says through her menu: "But you must have maple syrup."

David nudges her as Archie rolls his eyes. Andrew peeks over his menu to smile at the three and says: "I know what I'm having. Have the three of you made up your minds?"

Archie decides on the tomato soup, salad, and turkey sandwich. David texts to say he'll have the roast beef sandwich with corn soup. Nadine nods, ready. Andrew searches the restaurant for their waitress, and suddenly she's there at the end of their booth, order pad angled up, her pencil poised over it. Andrew gestures to Nadine who says: "I'll have the omelette with bacon and," she pauses, grins over at Archie, and continues: "with maple syrup." The waitress scribbles down their order, squinting at her pad through the lock of hair dangling in front of her eyes. She shakes it back as she lifts her head to take the next order. Andrew nods at Archie to go next; then he gives David and his orders. Andrew ends with: "We need creamer and sugar for our coffees."

"Oh, I'm so sorry. That gentleman over there made me forget. I'll go get them now for you." Their waitress slips her order pad and pencil into the pocket of her apron, hurries away, and returns with cream, milk, sugar, sweeteners, and creamers. She places the lot down on the centre of the table. "Enjoy your coffee. You need anything, you just holler. We here at Fran's are happy to have our troops here. Thank you so much!" she ends brightly, her lock of hair dancing in tune to her voice, making the men redden.

Nadine chortles and shakes her head. She reaches for the milk and sugar as the men look anywhere but at her.

"You guys are so easy," she teases. "A young thing thanks you, and you all go googly."

"What's googly?" Archie asks as he picks up his spoon to stir his coffee from hot to warm.

"Oh, you know," Nadine replies as she pours white crystals from the glass canister with its metal lid into the black, steaming liquid. She sets down the canister and picks up the milk jug and pours a steady stream, raising the level of coffee almost to the lip, almost matching it in colour to her white cup. She sets the jug down in the centre of the table and leans her head down to sip from the cup without having to move it and risk spilling more coffee. She slurps noisily. Nadine wants it all, every drop. She lifts her head and lifts her eyes: "Googly, you know. How you guys looked at her after she thanked us and all."

"Oh." He grabs the handle of his cup and lifts it towards her in a toast. The other three mimic him. "Here's to waitresses who make us men googly eyed and Nadine laugh again," Archie says.

"Here, here," the other three chorus, and they all slurp their coffees in unison then tuck in to their meals. Their chatter ripples out from their cozy booth, David's contributions appearing on Andrew, Nadine, and Archie's lock screens, their eyes automatically seeing them, their voices responding readily. Their banter mingles with the restaurant life swirling around but not touching them until "Happy birthday to you!" rings out. Customers turn as one towards the joyous sound. The waitress is carrying a cupcake with a candle driven in to its frosted top. Her hand guards its flickering flame as she walks to the lucky table.

Archie whispers, unbelieving he'd forgotten, "It's Stephen's birthday."

1345 HOURS

Chapter
14

"**I**T'S YOUR BIRTHDAY?" David messages Archie privately. Archie stares at the accusing words on his lock screen. Stephen's birthday. "When was the last time you spoke to your twin?" an invisible voice whispers. I'd like to forget, like Stephen had my birthday. Our birthday.

Archie pushes his plate of half-eaten apple pie toward Nadine, bumping his coffee cup. It's empty, and the waitress arrives at that moment to refill their cups. The other three pick their cups up and hold them out to make it easier for her to refill them. Archie leaves his cup in place. The waitress reaches past Andrew and refills his cup.

"Can't I get you heroes anything else?" she asks them brightly.

"Not right now. Coffee is fine," Andrew replies, raising his cup to her in thanks.

"Okay. Just holler if you need anything."

"Will do," Andrew assures her.

Andrew turns to David and cocks an eyebrow. David taps furiously on his iPhone, and all three are in a group message. "It's Archie's birthday."

Andrew slaps his forehead: "Oh my God, I forgot!"

Nadine lifts her head from her iPhone's screen and says: "Me too."

"We have to have cake," David messages the group.

Andrew nods and looks around for the waitress. He signals when she turns her head in their direction. "We have a birthday boy in our midst," he points to Archie, "and we went and forgot all about it. Can you do a little something for him?"

Archie half-raises a hand to say, "No, don't do anything," but the waitress is saying sprightly, "Of course," before he can voice his desire for avoidance. She disappears through the kitchen's swinging doors.

Archie frowns.

David messages: "Yeah, man, we're gonna do something. Suck it up."

Andrew laughs and slaps Archie on the back. "Looks like you have no choice."

Archie smiles with his mouth.

"Don't you have a twin?" Nadine asks.

"Yeah," Archie answers.

"What do you guys do, you know, twins, do you, like, wish each other happy birthday or something?"

Archie shakes his head. He's catching David's muteness. He clears his throat and answers: "No."

"No," Nadine says, nodding her head, "That'd be weird, eh?"

"Sometimes," Archie says, grinning despite himself as a fun memory surfaces.

"C'mon, tell us!" David messages Archie.

At that moment, the waitress arrives with the biggest chocolate cupcake with blue icing and white and red sprinkles on top. A single candle is lit, and its yellow flame wavers as she places it down on the table in front of Archie. The waitress begins to sing: "Happy birthday to you!" Andrew and Nadine join in as David messages Archie the merry song. Suddenly, the entire restaurant is singing along with the three, baritones underneath Nadine's resonant alto and female sopranos at the surrounding tables. A red tide swoops up Archie's neck, spreads along his chin and into his cheeks, branches out around his eyes, and flushes his forehead. His eyes glisten. The waitress chirrups: "Make a wish!" All the customers turn in their chairs to see what they can of Archie as he lowers his head with its spiky crown of black hair and blows once, hard, at the little flame. It flattens and then puffs out with a wisp of smoke.

The restaurant claps, and a couple of men shout: "Happy birthday, eh? Thanks for fighting for us!"

Archie nods in their general direction.

The waitress hurries off to see if the new customers who'd just walked in, shaking the rain off their coats, wanted some hot coffee to warm them up from the gale outside.

Archie's iPhone pings. He reads David's message. Archie lifts his deep brown eyes from the screen to David, fathomless in their depths of unsaid memories. He struggles to retrieve the happy memory, the one that had flown into his consciousness when Nadine had asked him, "Do you wish each other a happy birthday?"

"Yeah," Archie answers her question at last. "There was this one time." A rare look of mischief and glee crosses his face. He half-laughs.

"Yeah?" Andrew and Nadine prompt him in chorus as David joins them in leaning towards Archie.

Archie sits back. He picks up his fork and fiddles with it, smiling wickedly. He puts it down next to his cupcake plate at an odd angle, and Andrew's hand twitches. But he refrains from straightening it to lie exactly parallel to the plate.

Archie sits forward and pushes his cupcake plate slightly away to his right and leans his arms on the table. "Stephen was the firstborn."

"Yeah, we know that," Nadine says, her familiar impatience making Archie smile. He ducks his head and says: "Yeah, okay."

David messages the group: "Let him tell his story."

Nadine berates David good-humouredly, "Hey! If I want to interrupt, I can. I'm his superior, okay?"

David holds up both his hands in surrender.

Nadine turns back to Archie and makes a winding motion with her right hand: "Go on."

Archie draws in a silent breath, suddenly not sure if he can. Andrew grins strength at him as he grips his shoulder. "Tell the story in your own time, Archie."

The supportive warmth from Andrew's large, meaty hand soaks into Archie. Suddenly, he wants to remember that happy memory. "As I was saying," Archie begins with a significant look from his smiling eyes. Nadine grins back. "As you were saying, Archie?"

"Yeah, as I was saying, Stephen is my older brother, as he likes to remind me. He was the firstborn. By two minutes," Archie holds his first two fingers up in the V-for-Victory sign. "He came out wailing, Ma said. But I came out silent like a lamb."

Nadine snorts: "You, a lamb?"

Archie takes on a mock serious expression: "Yes, ma'am. Me."

Nadine shakes her head and chuckles.

Archie huffs and continues: "I was the silent as a lamb one. Pawpaw gave me all the good stuff on our birthdays because of that. He figured I needed boosting up cause all the attention went to Stephen, the eldest one. He'll inherit the house, Sir used to say. I figured he could have the house. It was run down, paint peeling all over the place, and there was only one toi-let." Archie draws the corners of his lips down.

Nadine shudders. "All those males and only one toilet? How'd your mother survive?"

"She made do."

"I feel for her, I really do."

"Hey!" David messages Nadine. "We're well behaved."

Nadine turns to David and informs him: "That's cause I trained you."

Male laughter surrounds her. Nadine raises her eyebrows at them. "It's true."

"Not for me," Archie retorts. "Ma taught me properly, taught us twins properly."

"Okay, okay." Nadine gives in, with a half-grin, but her eyes say she isn't giving a millimetre on her claim.

"Anyway, as I was say-ing." Archie angles his chest forward a little and settles onto his forearms, relaxing on the table. "It was our ninth birthday. I woke up first. Stephen always woke up first. But I did that time. I went into the kitchen where Ma was making us our special birthday pancakes and cooking up a pile of bacon for us all. Pawpaw was already there with his present for me wrapped up in a box. He and Ma were arguing cause Pawpaw hadn't gotten Stephen one. They didn't see me. Stephen had lorded it over me all year about him having better marks, him being more popular with the kids, the teachers liking him better cause he was smart and I was dumb. Pawpaw was saying I needed to feel special. Ma was saying he needed to treat us the same. 'No one else does,' Pawpaw shouted, and slammed his fist down on our table. Ma jumped, and I scurried away before she saw me lurking there in the doorway. I scrambled back into bed and watched Stephen pretend sleeping.

"I knew he was awake cause he always did this stretching thing like Sir did, like he was a man. Stephen was no man. My twin was a boy like me. And Pawpaw had gotten me a present but not him. He didn't know it yet. When he looked over at me, I grinned and laughed. 'What's so funny?' he says. He hated not knowing what I knew. And I knew something he didn't. 'Happy birthday,' I shot back. Stephen got all magnanimous like he was the one with favour not me and trying to look like he didn't care I knew something he didn't. 'Happy birthday,' he said, bowing his head like he was some kind of king. So like we get up and go into the kitchen. You could hear Stephen coming a mile away. He wanted everyone to know when he was coming and when he was in the room. Not me. The louder he got, the quieter I got. You find out things when people don't hear you coming."

"Or hear you standing there," Nadine interrupts mildly.

Archie nods and continues: "So Stephen, he spots Pawpaw's gift, the box with the bright blue paper with cowboys and guns all over it. He goes over to grab that present, and Pawpaw he whips it away from him. He says, 'Not for you, son. This is for Archie.' Pawpaw hands it to me, right in front of Stephen. You shoulda seen Stephen's face. His jaw dropped, he was that shocked. For an entire year, no one minded me, they all gave him things and ignored me. But that birthday, it was the opposite. I said, 'Happy birthday' to Stephen again, stuck my tongue out at him, and opened the present right in front of him. He was maa-ad." Archie's eyes shine with the blackness of remembered one-upmanship, one of the few times he'd triumphed over his twin.

"Revenge was sweet, eh?" Nadine says.

"Yeah. And I didn't even make it happen."

"But you took advantage of it?"

Archie nods, his lips straightening out from his grin, his eyebrows' inner ends wrinkling up. Nadine says: "It made you feel good. Did it last?"

Archie's eyes flatten into matte black-brown discs. "No."

Nadine nods. She says: "Revenge never does. But the moment your grandfather tried to balance out the attention for you was good. That moment lasted?"

Archie looks at the cupcake and its candle with its wick burnt black, a couple of drips of white wax stark on the blue icing. "Yes." Archie breathes for a few seconds. "Pawpaw always tried to even out the balance." He looks up at them. "Right to the day I enlisted. He left me his gun. It was the only thing he trusted, and he trusted me with it. He didn't let Stephen ever touch it. But Pawpaw taught me. He taught me how to hold it, how to pull its trigger, how to load it, how to shoot it. He let me clean it the last year of his life. We went target shooting with that gun every weekend, every Friday after school, after that birthday. I had to get good grades to go on Friday shoots with him. He said he wanted me to do better than him, to ignore my parents saying I could never be as good as Stephen. He knew I could be as good as I wanted to be and whatever that was, was good enough for him. But I had to stretch myself. 'No laying about, Archie!'" Archie laughs mirthlessly. "Pawpaw was smart. He didn't rely on my word. He taught me, 'Trust the word and back it up with checking.' That's how my word became trustworthy. You never know when you'll be back checked. Yeah, Pawpaw was good. He demanded to see my tests and report cards. Yeah, Pawpaw took care of me." Archie falls silent. The other three sit with him, their sorrow for him stretching around him like a comforting blanket of energy. They know the story he's now tumbling into. He'd told them that day in Afghanistan, the day he'd first relived his righteous shoot.

1415 HOURS

Chapter 15

As the four veterans leave Fran's, Andrew puts a hand on Archie's arm to delay him, letting David and Nadine walk ahead in the rain that's started up again. Andrew asks Archie, as he lets go of Archie: "Is Nadine's ex a threat?"

The two men walk side by side, Archie breathing in the rain-freshened city air.

"He thinks we're having an affair, sir."

"Are you?" Andrew asks, keeping his eyes ahead as they walk east along College towards Yonge Street and their favourite pub downtown for David's annual drink.

"No, sir," Archie shakes his head, rain drops flying off the spikes of his hair. He remembers the Tilley hat in his hand and puts it on his head, pulling the rim down with both hands. The Canadian-made hat fits snugly, and the sudden gust of wind that blows rain horizontally into their backs cannot budge it.

Andrew nods and pulls up his collar against the whipping rain. "I didn't think so, but I wanted to check. To deal with a situation, we must have all the facts."

"Yes, sir."

"Is he bothering Nadine?"

"I don't believe so, sir. But he is a threat."

"How so?"

"He came at me in the middle of the night. Tried to break down my door. He came at me after the service, too. Tried to assault me. He might've had a weapon."

Andrew twists his head to look at Archie, but the rim of the Tilley hat hides Archie's eyes from the taller man. Andrew asks the hat, with an edge in his voice: "Did he?"

Archie frowns and considers the sidewalk. "I'm not sure. He might've."

"Did you see one?"

Archie squints up at the sky, trying to recall, the wind sharpening his focus on the here and now. The rain cools his face. "I don't think I saw one." He pauses and adds reluctantly: "No."

Andrew bends slightly, his eyes locking onto Archie's temporarily visible ones: "You must always ascertain the threat's intention. If he doesn't have a weapon, proceed with caution, but know you have the upper hand. Don't draw yours."

"I didn't, sir."

Andrew stares at Archie appraisingly. "You have it?"

"Yes, sir," Archie answers, stiffening his back, growing taller, keeping his face angled upward, looking Andrew square in the eye. "Always. It's protection."

Andrew challenges mildly: "Is it?"

Archie doesn't change expression. "Always. Sir."

"We're in Toronto. In Canada, not in Afghanistan any more. There are other ways to deal with threats."

"Where I come from, sir, we know how to solve our problems. We're used to threat assessment."

"Here, we're used to a different way of thinking. Threats are enemies. Nadine and her ex are human beings in pain. We don't solve pain with a gun."

Archie blinks. Pawpaw's blasted-off face bullets into his mind's eye and commands his emotions with all the force of an IED. His stomach clenches. Breath leaves him, and he rasps like a worn-out horse. Archie swallows hard against the hot bile exploding into his throat, trying to hide his flashback. But Andrew's narrowed eyes tell him he hasn't succeeded. Andrew says gently: "You're here in Toronto, Specialist. You're here in a peaceful city with your friends. Tell me where we are."

"In Toronto, sir," Archie replies woodenly, his grandfather's final solution spraying his heart, extinguishing the fire for life out of him. Torment eats his cells.

Archie cannot breathe.

Andrew grabs his shoulder with his solid hand. He steers Archie to stand against the nearest brick building. Andrew doesn't crowd him but stands close, letting his body shield him from the rain and the people walking and shoving around them. "Specialist, look at me. Will I let anything happen to you?"

Archie shoots his eyes over Andrew's left shoulder, his right shoulder. Andrew's voice lowers into a soothing purr. "It's okay, Specialist. We're in a peaceful country now. We're not where you are."

"No, sir," Archie says as his father's accusations barrel through his head. "You're responsible for your grandfather's death. You're the young one, you should've been protecting him. You always were a coward. Old men don't die like that. Someone must've shot him. Where's his gun?" The accusations reverberate against Archie's struggle to shove those words out of his mind.

"What are you remembering, Archie? Tell me."

Archie opens his mouth. The words remain locked in his brain. He swallows. He tries again. His voice engages hoarsely, and the story spills out. Andrew stands impassively, saying nothing until Archie winds down. Then he states: "Your father was wrong."

Archie's eyes fill; tears waterfall. Andrew fishes in his pants pocket and pulls out a packet of tissues. He pulls one tissue out and hands it to Archie, shifting his body to allow Archie to keep his dignity away from the prying eyes of strangers. Archie wipes his eyes hard with the thick tissue. The tissue gleams against his skin in the dim light of the rain. He blows his nose and stuffs the tissue in his jacket pocket, no longer able to smell anything. "Thank you, sir."

"No problem, Specialist."

Archie nods.

Andrew asks: "Are you here now?"

"Yes, sir, yes, I am."

Andrew smiles. "Good." He claps him on the shoulder. And the two resume their walk south on Yonge Street as they unhurriedly follow David and Nadine. "We'll talk about threat assessment in Canada's largest city. But first, a drink."

"Yes, sir."

1503 HOURS

Chapter 16

ARCHIE FOLLOWS ANDREW through the pub's traditional wooden double entrance doors with their small square window panes in their top halves. They remove their hat and beret, shaking raindrops onto the floor of black-stained oak. A path bleached from many feet leads the silent men across wide planks to where David and Nadine are standing at the blackened bar that stretches along the back wall of the pub. Wear marks streak its surface, and behind it a mirror reflects the black-painted ceiling with its pinpoints of light illuminating the bar in a series of pools. Through the mirror, Archie scans the entrance and the three rectangular windows on either side of the double doors, with their black mullions. Satisfied his vantage point allows him to spot any threats, he shifts his focus to the glass shelves lining the mirror, which hold bottles of vodka, gin, vermouth, whisky, all the hard liquor a man who wants to forget his internal nightmares could want. They order beer—"the usual"—in answer to David's message: "What are you having?"

David messages the bartender, who's polishing glasses down at the other end of the bar. The bartender puts a glass down, retrieves his massive Samsung from his pocket, checks it, nods at David, and serves them their beers.

Andrew has a brown bottle of Molson Blue.

Nadine has her half pint of Lager poured into a thick glass mug.

David has a full pint of Bitter in a clean tall glass, scratched and clouded with heavy use.

Archie has his "piss brew," as the Canadians used to joke on the base. "We have to get it specially trucked in for you, Specialist," they'd mock-tell-him-off as they banged his bottle down in front of him. Archie got used to the ribbing. They say nothing now. In silence, they pick up their bottles and glasses and carry them down the length of the pub, past the end of the bar, past a workstation, to a table kept empty and waiting for them in the pub's far corner away from any windows. Judiciously placed planters and the workstation that remains unused while they jaw at their table, protect the four from the other customers. They scrape their chairs back and crowd around the plain black-veneer table, placing their beer, tan Tilley hat, and army green berets on its top. They unbutton their outside jackets or dress jackets but don't remove them.

David used to spend his days here, sitting at the collegial bar on his better days, but mostly at this lonely table, turning his glass round and round in his roughened hands. *Yet he, weirdly enough,* thinks Archie, *didn't get addicted to alcohol.*

Archie scans the premises while he remembers how David had liked to sit and drink and drink and watch others drink or talk so that he didn't have to think or talk to anyone. But then one day he saw his half-empty glass with its rim of foam sinking down to the pale golden liquid and disgust had overcome him. He'd shoved it away, the glass sliding to the edge of the round table with its scarring of rim marks. The glass had teetered there. David didn't rescue it. Instead, he'd barged his chair back, picked up his jacket, slung it over his shoulders, and moved. He'd brushed his glass with the hem of his jacket, and the glass had thrown itself to the floor. That's how David had described it to them. It was like it had acted out what David had been doing. A passing waitress had quickly reached out a hand and grabbed it in mid-suicide. David took that as a sign and had banged out the bar. He didn't return for an entire year. Then, on Remembrance Day, he'd told his buddies it was time for one drink. They'd joined him. When Archie had arrived in Canada, he'd tagged along and was told the story as David had his one drink and the other three joined him. And then they had, one by one, related the stories that haunted them the most. David had insisted on this ritual. "Time to spill it instead of drink it and have it bloat up our bellies," he'd messaged. Archie had resisted participating in that part of the ritual, but today David messages him: "Time to fess up, Specialist."

Archie shakes his head and ducks it down to stare into the neck of his bottle. Archie's left hand cradles the bottle's body as his right hand, leaning on the table, holds his iPhone face up. David huffs beside him. Nadine says: "Never mind him, David. We'll go first. He can go last. The wait will do him good."

Archie doesn't react as David grunts. A message pings his iPhone, and Archie slides his eyes towards it. "After Nadine, you're up. No escaping this year." Archie says nothing, only shifts his eyes back to his bottle, then leans back, letting the iPhone fall from his lax fingers onto the table with a muted clatter, as he lets his momentum lift the bottle to his lips to take a long pull of the cold, bland liquid. He swallows hard. The other three watch him, concern writ over Andrew's face. Nadine steals a glance at Andrew and puts a bright expression on her face. She says: "Captain, I have a story you don't want to hear."

Her voice distracts Andrew's attention from Archie; his eyebrows fly up into his hair: "What?"

"The day the fish fried itself."

Andrew's mouth drops open, then suddenly he hoots: "Nadine, you come up with the most outrageous—Okay, I'll bite. Tell me about the day the fish fried itself."

"It was so tired of swimming up the cold river, jumping high into the cold air only to land in colder water that when it saw the fire on the land and the steam rising from the pot, it said to itself, now that looks better and jumped over the bank. But it missed the pot and landed in the fry pan."

Archie spews beer and bangs the bottle on the table. Andrew guffaws and leans back in his chair so far that suddenly his arms are windmilling and his booted feet are searching for purchase on the floor. David grins. Archie lunges and grabs his commander's arm, his body shaking with laughter, while Nadine sits and watches, cat-like satisfaction purring all over her face. Archie saves Andrew from collapsing backwards on the floor. "Alright, sir?" he chokes out between laughs.

Andrew nods, grinning: "Yes, Archie, I am. Thank you." He turns to Nadine as Archie wipes his mouth from the beer that spilled on to his chin. "You!"

Nadine grins at him. "Yes, sir, I'm guilty sir."

Andrew laughs and claps her on the shoulder. "Well done, Sergeant, well done."

Nadine nods and says: "Thank you, sir. Always at your service."

"That you are, Sergeant. The best damn Sergeant I ever had. You always have my back."

Nadine's grin shows teeth, her blue eyes darken, and the wrinkles on the outside edges disappear. Andrew claps her again as he turns his attention to Archie. "I believe you owe us a story, Specialist."

Archie points his bottle at Nadine. "Her first." He looks at her with a knowing look. Nadine lifts her cheeks to extend her grin. "Whatever you say. You always needed some courage time."

Archie quirks his mouth into a wry smile. Three iPhones ping at the same time. "He never lacked for courage Nadine"

Nadine pulls her mouth down. "You're right, David. I'm sorry, Archie. You were the best damn American who ever served with us. You could keep up."

Archie laughed sourly.

"It's true," Nadine insisted. "You earned our respect."

"She's right," Andrew says, pointing the neck of his bottle at Archie, before taking a long swallow.

Archie nods.

Their iPhones ping again. "You first, Nadine. No avoiding it either."

Nadine reads her screen and nods. "Alright, David, alright." She picks up her glass mug, drinks deeply, sets it carefully down on the table, holds it with her right hand for a long moment, then abruptly lets go. "It was that day of the firefight. We were walking in formation behind the wall. You remember those walls, made of pale mud to go with that pale landscape that we all stood out against like sitting targets in the range." The other three nod. "I remember the tree. There was this tree with this thin trunk and branches that didn't know where to go. Green leaves made it stand out. Green against all that paleness." The men lean their forearms on the table, each cradling his beer in his right hand, their iPhones resting together on the table. Their eyes glue to Nadine's face. Nadine drops her eyes to her mug. She touches it, turning it round and round with her fingertips, then grabs it. Nadine lifts her beer and swallows hard, making a moue of distaste as she puts it back down. "It was that tree that stuck in my mind." The air hushes around her as she stares at her beer. It, too, waits for her to tell her story in her own time. The three men know this story. They know what comes next. She's told it before. Briefly, Archie feels that it's a cover, that the story she wants to tell, the story that'll free her, remains locked in her breast, behind bars of fear, fear of hearing her lips and tongue form dreaded words out loud, fear of how they, the men, will react, fear of revealing a secret she doesn't want to be real, fear of what change will come from revealing that secret.

Archie briefly thinks about asking her to tell that story instead.

The question scrolls across his mind: *Nadine, why not tell the story you're most afraid to tell? That's why we're here.* His heart beats a tattoo of "don't tell, don't tell, don't tell," like her heart must be ordering her to do. She's listening to her heart; he wonders if he will, if he will, like her, tell a well-worn story, one that sounds like the stuff of hell that lives in the nightmares and daymares, but in fact has been reconciled, has been shorn of its horror in the light of retelling to companions who don't judge but empathize, who nod their understanding and hug out their compassion for each other, soothing each other's wounds. Their empathy means never having to say sorry for telling the same story for the umpteenth time.

Some wounds hurt too much for talk to soothe.

Archie leaves his thoughts and returns to the present reality. Nadine is saying: "...It was the blood. I didn't expect the blood to spatter up on the wall like an abstract painting I saw once in the National Gallery." The men nod; they know she's referring to her high school trip when her art teacher had taken her class to the National Art Gallery in Ottawa to learn about abstract expressionism. "All I could think about at the time is, he painted in blood." Nadine falls silent. The others remain in silence with her. Slowly, Andrew reaches out his right arm and encircles her shoulders with it. David reaches across the table with his left hand and clasps hers that's lying on the table. Archie sits there, unable to move.

He doesn't want to hear what his mind is telling him he sees in Nadine.

David kicks Archie's booted foot under the table. Hard. Archie doesn't acknowledge it by so much as a twitch in his body; instead he reaches out his own left hand to place it on top of Nadine's left wrist. They sit like this for long moments until Nadine sighs, shifts her body back into her chair, and lifts her mug with her right hand. The three men settle back into their places.

Nadine bangs her mug down. "Your turn," she says to Archie, her darkened blue eyes looking straight into his shadowed brown ones, both knowing but refusing to know what the other is thinking.

Archie hears himself say: "It was the righteous shoot." Andrew and David sit up, surprised. Nadine nods. Archie clenches his teeth together. He stares into his bottle, shocked at hearing those words out loud. Andrew says: "Go on."

"It was the righteous shoot," Archie tells his bottle. "It was back in my unit, the Fifth Brigade Combat Team."

The other three hold their breath, don't move even though all three want to take long pulls at their beer. Saliva vanishes from their mouths.

Archie starts speaking, word by word. "We were in a convoy, moving fast. My commanding officer was sitting next to me, ordering me to go faster. I had my foot jammed against the accelerator. I didn't know how speed could outmanoeuvre an IED, but my commanding officer...he knew better than I did. I hadn't been there long. He'd been on three tours by then. He knew all about the people. I was still learning. He told me I knew nothing. This was not America and stop being a pussy. Pussy, his favourite word. Pussy this. Pussy that. He'd shut us up with that word. He'd get us to obey him with that word. No man wants to be a pussy." Archie jams the bottle against his lips and suctions beer into his mouth. He chokes and gulps. He suspends the bottle partway back down to the table. "Speed mattered. If you didn't react fast enough, you were dead. If you didn't drive fast enough, you were dead. He didn't want to be dead. And he didn't need no pussy making him dead neither. That's what he said."

Archie lifts his bottle back to his lips. He swallows half the beer convulsively. He places it soundlessly on the table and continues: "So anyway, I drove. I drove so fast, I couldn't see far enough down the road to know where it was going. The curves were hair raising. Sometimes I thought we'd tip over. I slowed down once so as not to, and he yelled so loud, I thought my ear drum would pop." The other three wonder at the lungs of his old superior, for the engines of those LAVs were deafening. The whine must've been like a shell forever coming at him, forever hanging over him. But they don't shake their heads in understanding. The three barely breathe. They don't want Archie to stop. They know of the righteous shoot, but that's all he'd ever said: "righteous shoot." They only know it'd been the source of friction between him and his family, but they know nothing about it. Today, the story is escaping out of his heart's locked box. They want to be there for him fully in soul and heart as he's telling it.

Archie continues: "So I'm racing down this road, go round this bend in that godforsaken landscape of hell, and suddenly this man is standing there. I run right over him. Right over him. And I can't even feel him underneath my wheels. I can't hear anything, the engine is so loud. I jam on the brakes and—," emotion catches up to Archie. His voice changes from deadpan to broken. He doesn't clear his throat but lets the grief quaver his voice, for he must tell it. Now it's released, the memory demands the light. "My commanding officer, he asks me, 'What're you doing? You don't brake, Private. You drive.' I go, 'But I hit a man.' He says, 'So what? They're the enemy.' I go, 'I don't know that sir, I got to see him.' I've braked the LAV and am opening the door at this point. My commanding officer is having a fit. His face is all red, and I'm worried he's going to pop an artery or something, But I need to see that man, even if he's going to have me up for treason. Maybe he's alive, I was thinking. He looked old. I run to the back of my LAV and there he is all mangled and everything. And his beard—," Archie chokes on a rising sob. "His beard is all white!" Archie's voice rises in remembered horror. "He's an old man. My commanding officer, he's behind me and he's dragging me back to the vehicle by my collar. But I'm younger and stronger and pull myself out of his grip. I squat down to feel for a pulse. But the driver of the LAV behind us comes up to me and tells me he's dead. 'You gotta get off the road,' he says. He had no emotion. There's an old man, dying in front of us, and he's talking like we're at a fender bender. He says, 'Otherwise they'll kill us. We got to keep moving.' But I wanted to move this old man to the side of the road. I refuse my officer's order to get back in the LAV and drive on. So the other driver and me, we pick him up. I didn't expect him to be so heavy or to bend so, so—," Archie gags as the others remember what it's like to move a human body that's been broken into pieces. Archie drags in a breath, steadying his voice. His right hand rises involuntarily to his mouth. He speaks through his closed fingers. "I didn't know what it was like to move a broken body. It was my first one. The driver kept looking around, saying we got to hurry before the others come. 'They all have guns, you know,' he told me. 'They'll shoot on sight. Soon as they see we killed one of their elders, they'll be gunning for us. Hurry up, man.' But I couldn't move faster. My legs were lead. Time was like nothing. No time existed. I could only creep forward. I couldn't carry or walk normally. This old man's blood was dripping all over my hands, and his torso was bending this way and that. It wasn't natural, and I wanted to scream. But I'd been trained, and Sir, my father, said, men don't scream. No crying either. I couldn't let the others see I was crying. So I blinked hard. I'd dropped my end of the old man's b— b— body. The other driver, he kept hold of his feet. They were still intact. His legs were bending the wrong way. I picked up his shoulders again, and they went kind of squirrelly in my hands, but I just shut my senses down and told myself I had to go faster. My commanding officer had gone back to the LAV, but it was like I could still hear him shouting: 'They'll kill us if you don't get moving. Faster, Private, faster. Pussy!'" Archie's arm slackens; his hand falls away from his mouth. Moments pass while time holds its breath.

"So's anyway, we get him to the side of the road, and the driver says, 'Let's move.' And I say, 'No, I need to say a prayer.' He snorts, 'A prayer, in this hellhole, for who?' 'Him!' I shout, pointing down at the old man all covered in dust and blood. You can hardly see his beard is white anymore. The driver...he shook his head and says, 'Okay, but hurry up.' We bow our heads and close our eyes, like we were taught. I say something quick, I don't know what, just asking God to save him and forgive me. I look up first, and I see this young tall man, coming at us real quick. He's got an angry look on his face, like he's going to kill us. His hands are free, but all I see is that anger. 'Look out!' I yell as I push the other driver away, reach for my combat pistol, pull it, and shoot. I'm real accurate. Pawpaw made sure of that. He went down in one shot. I run towards him to make sure he's dead. I'd hit him dead centre between the eyes. His eyes are flat. No life in him, either. The driver comes up to me, shakes my hand for saving his life, and that's when I see that...that...that...." Archie deflates. His chest concaves; his neck loses strength; and his head drops. Archie whispers, "The man had no weapon on him. I searched his garments, thinking I'd seen him reach for one, but there's nothing in all that clothing, those tent-like things they wear, those clothes I'd been told over and over they wear to hide their weapons. 'You gotta watch out for them. They're sneaky,' they'd all said. But that young guy, he'd been angry, and that was all. Who wouldn't be if your grandfather had been hit and was lying there all broken up? I was frozen. The driver, he pulled me up, told me if we didn't get going, we'd have to shoot all the villagers, and he points into the distance. That's when I look down the road and see them. People are coming at us. I can't have more death. So's I run back to the LAV and drive the hell out of there. My commanding officer didn't have to tell me to gun it. 'Good work, Private,' he yells. He congratulates me. 'You got two of them. That'll get you a medal.' He didn't shout at me the whole rest of the day, just sat back smiling like the proverbial cat, telling me what a righteous shoot it was, how I'd saved their lives, how I'd rid the world of one more Tal-i-ban and one more terr-orist. They toasted me that night. We all got drunk. I got drunk every night after that."

<u>1659 HOURS</u>

Chapter
17

ARCHIE CALLS OUT goodbye as he turns left away from the other three, who are turning right. After Archie had revealed the details of his righteous shoot, the others had sat with him in silence and then...

Archie doesn't remember what happened next. He grasps at tendrils of memory drifting into the soaked clouds of his mind. David had finished his beer and texted them all a short story about his first day in Afghanistan. He and the troops he was with had driven straight from the airport to the base, listening to warnings about IEDs. The ones who'd already done one tour related to the new troops the fears they'd have to learn to live with: the fear of being blown up at any moment, without warning, without a siren or whistle to tell them what was about to happen. Andrew, Nadine, and Archie had nodded in recognition of that experience. "Kaboom!" The word showing up on their screens simultaneously had made the three jump.

Kaboom. The word reverberates in Archie's mind. It won't leave. It repeats over and over and over like a mental bad burrito that won't digest itself. Like a burrito that sits in his gut waiting for what he doesn't know. Archie refuses to eat burritos anymore. Ever since that day, the day of—

Archie shakes his head. He'd told his story. He'd told it to his family, his VA counsellor, and now his Canadian platoon. But he doesn't want to remember it, think about it, or feel it anymore.

Archie stretches his neck up and inhales noisily through his nose. The rain has stopped. Sun gleams feebly on the puddles in the road. A car hisses by, its tires surfing the water, throwing a wave that catches a woman, head down over her smartphone, unaware. The water splashes the left side of her black puffy coat with its belt cinching in her tiny waist, but she keeps walking, her back screaming how intent she is on the phone in her hand as the water drips off the hem of her coat, like the blood dripping off the man as he carried—

A sob grabs Archie's gullet, and bile retches his throat. He struggles not to vomit all over the black road next to him shining with the fresh water that had poured from the sky and pooled over the asphalt. He wants to ruin its transparent clarity with the puke of his memory. Archie swallows and keeps walking, stuffing his hands into his pockets to bring them comfort, to feel with his left the hidden protection of his Sig.

Andrew had spoken his story next. Andrew's resilient, tough and resilient, like many of the Canadian officers he'd met over there. None of them shouted, their vocal cords stiff with fear and loathing like his Combat Team commander had in that nightmare LAV for mile after mile of pale sandy ribbon in that rocky, mountainous landscape. Andrew's story was like a soothing balm on them all. Yet Archie was aware that Andrew feels responsible for all three of them. Andrew's grief at failing his troops who'd died was palpable; grief had flowed from his eyes and dripped down his cheeks.

Andrew, a big man with broad shoulders and a thick neck, with an open face and a wide smile, with a straight stance and trunk-like trees, had no shame in crying openly in a pub where anyone could see him.

Archie envies him his grief. Andrew's grief sits there like Lake Ontario, so enormous, it cannot be denied, so easy to see that he can ask for help and receive it. Andrew's in counselling. He wants them all to be in counselling. Only Archie isn't. Counselling is helping Andrew, but the others...

Besides, he revealed it all to his VA counsellor, even more than what he'd told them today over beer. And then his counsellor had left. Just like that. Not a word, not a warning. All bared; gone.

I won't do that again, Archie vows. *I won't share my shame and then be left standing there, alone again.*

After Andrew's story, the four veterans had pushed back their chairs, the scraping noisy in the small, separated area; had buttoned up their jackets; and marched out. Andrew and David were taking Nadine back home. The two men are concerned about her, as is Archie. But he can't support anyone right now. Archie's frozen within himself in his thoughts and emotions. Andrew and David had wanted him to accompany them.

Archie wants to be alone.

Archie knows alone.

Alone comforts in familiarity and no expectations of support.

As he walks forward, hunched into himself, his eyes scan the people strolling, walking, hurrying towards him, away from him. Archie's senses stretch around him on either side as his peripheral vision takes in those who pass by him too closely. His ears hear the pounding of many feet behind him and the splashing of cars as they speed towards and past him on his left.

Archie's vigilance doesn't falter.

Archie's vigilance robs his energy as it hoses endless information into his brain.

Archie stumbles and lurches into an alley. He crashes against the graffiti-clad wall, floundering into boxes and wooden crates lying in the crease between the old brick wall and the pot-marked alleyway. Hands plant themselves on his back, and Archie lurches again. He falls. His fingers touch the rough broken asphalt beneath his unsure feet. His abdominal muscles clench, keep him from splatting, and he half-runs, half-crawls away from the unforeseen and unseen threat behind him. But the threat is on top of him. Something long and hard hits his back, thwacking him flat on the ground. A battered bin on wheels on one side and littered pieces of wooden crates on the other side prevent him from rolling over. *How much garbage fills this alley? The threat chose well.* A board slams against the asphalt next to his face, spattering his eyes and nose with dirt. Archie scrambles forward; hands and feet propel him into the space behind the bin. He half falls into paper-filled boxes, crushing them with his weight, their wet papers making him slide forwards, almost hitting the wall with his head. The threat's angry feet dance towards him. Using his powerful abdominal muscles, Archie launches himself upright. He kicks the boxes violently to the side, clearing a square of asphalt, and turns swiftly so that he's facing the threat. Archie plants his legs firmly apart, ready to spring at the threat, raises his fists, poises to strike, to lunge at the threat's head. For now, he chooses to use the hand-to-hand combat skills he perfected while embedded in his Canadian unit.

Archie hasn't forgotten his protection: his Sig Sauer P320, loaded and ready to eliminate the threat with one squeeze of the trigger, requiring no time to take a safety off. But he's decided almost unconsciously against using the combat pistol his commanding officer in the Combat Team had handed him on his first day in his tour of duty. "Take this," his superior had compelled. "That gun will be your best friend, the extra protection you're gonna need in this fucking hellhole." Archie had been unsure—surely, the army had equipped him fully with all that he needed. But the US Army's training had prepared him to obey orders, and after a brief hesitation that had elicited a glare, he'd snatched the gun. He'd obeyed his superior in modifying the gun's sights to suit his shooting. Obeyed him in practicing with targets until he was as accurate with it as with his other guns. Obeyed right up to ending that unarmed man's life on the road.

Archie's commanding officer had approved. Yet had instructed him not to let anyone outside the platoon know about his extra combat pistol, to ensure they didn't know the man was unarmed because, his commanding officer had informed him while his eyes held his in an overbright stare, the man had concealed his weapon. Archie just hadn't found it. The weapon had been there on the road. The other driver had spotted it. Archie had missed it, is all. "I don't remember him doing that, sir. I didn't miss seeing it, I'm sure, sir," Archie had said. His commanding officer had repeated, his nose almost touching Archie's, that the driver had spotted it, that Archie had forgotten, and that he was to tell no one outside the platoon of his doubts. "Understood, Private?" Archie had felt hypnotized, unable to nod or to say yes.

Night after night, the platoon had regaled themselves with their righteous shoot. The platoon's approval, when he'd finally agreed with them, contrasted warmly against their hostility when he'd first expressed his regret and remorse. They'd flayed him and forced him to stay up every night guarding their position until sleep deprivation had made him hallucinate. Maybe they were right, and he was wrong, he'd begun to think.

"Was it a righteous shoot?" his commanding officer had bellowed at him in his morning ritual in front of the rest of the men. "Did the man you shot have a weapon?"

"Yes, sir," Archie had replied.

"I can't hear you!" his superior had bellowed, leaning into Archie's face.

"Yes sir!" Archie had shouted back, and his heart had leadened inside him.

Archie'd slept for 15 hours, and they'd let him. The cook had made him a full breakfast with extra rashers of bacon when he'd woken up, and they'd rewarded him by excusing him from guard duty for two weeks after that and by rigging up a satellite connection so that he could speak to his family that night. Archie had related the story to his family, like a man repeating a script at gunpoint. He'd expected Sally to be horrified. Instead, Sally had said she finally had something to lord it over the other wives. Her husband had made a righteous shoot and deserved a medal. She was going to make sure he got that medal. Sir, leaning over her shoulder to stare right into the camera, had crowed over his triumph over the Tal-i-ban. The last of Archie's doubts had drowned in their praise. Archie's heart had disappeared behind bunkers. The pistol had transformed itself from a thing of horror to a thing of comfort. The pistol had become Archie's weapon of experience and choice.

Archie blinks.

The threat is spitting on Archie's lips, he's yelling so hard.

The threat is the ex.

Nadine's ex.

Archie frowns. He'd gotten rid of him.

Apparently not.

Nadine's ex is here.

Archie's failure at eliminating this threat confuses him and makes him drop his hands.

The ex leans into Archie, his face almost nose-to-nose with his face. Somehow, his hands pinion Archie's upper arms against the wall, and his right leg inserts between Archie's own two splayed-out ones. The ex's knee hovers in a dangerous position. Archie stills himself, sends his rage and eternal memories into a far-off place, and focuses on the threat in front of him. Archie curses himself for allowing his memories to drown his awareness, for letting his vigilance grow into ineffectiveness.

Never let your guard down.

Not even in civvie land.

Discriminate between priorities, and eliminate from vigilance what's not important.

Archie hadn't, and now he could die.

Archie isn't sure that's not a bad thing.

Death would release him. And the ex would get the rap, he's so sloppy.

Visual, auditory, olfactory senses vibrate him with information. They're in the alley alone; his stumbling momentum had taken them halfway down. Clouds drip onto them. Archie shifts his gaze to the grey-lit rectangle at the end of the alley. People are lifting their collars, popping open their umbrellas, not paying attention to the two men in the alley as they hurry to their destinations. For them, the two men between the two walls, surrounded by filth and litter, are just another fighting couple, nothing to do with them. *But her ex will leave clues all over the place, Archie muses, and the police will find him soon after they find my body.*

A two-fer, Archie thinks.

Win-win.

Archie relaxes at the thought. His muscles flab into softness underneath his jacket, under the ex's hands.

The ex frowns. Nadine's ex is sober now, but his fury of revenge flames on. He must blame someone else. He must punish this man who's responsible for this intolerable failure with Nadine. And suddenly this man doesn't care?

Outrage bellows out of him. Incoherent words lash Archie's cheeks.

Archie isn't listening. His mind floats backwards, away from the alley and the rage. From his peaceful place of detachment, Archie regards the ex's bulging eyes, their whites ribboned with red, his cheeks flushed purple through veins that brighten then darken as more and more blood course in. Anger intensifies his irises' colour. Archie wonders what colour they are. Archie retreats farther; reality becomes a far-off play of shadows.

The ex slams him against the wall's age-roughened bricks, screaming, "You poached my girl, you filthy American! I'm going to give you what you're owed. You can't do nothing about it now because I'm the one in control now, see?! I won't let you get away with cheating, right under my nose! I'm going to make you pay! You thought you were so clever. You think you're stronger than me. Look at you now! Who's got the upper hand, huh?"

Archie's left shoulder drops further, his arm slackens, and his hand brushes against the grip hidden underneath his jackets. The polymer composite hard grip stuns his palm.

"I have you right where I want you! You can't do nothing, you lowlife American punk!"

Messages from his palm collide with messages from his ears. Nerves carry the ex's screams and the touch of his pistol into his brain. The pistol's hardness slingshots Archie back into present reality and the ex's saliva decorating his face. *The pistol is who you are,* his Sig seems to declare.

Archie thrusts himself upright, raises his hands upward and inward, and powers them outward with a great roar from deep within his lungs. The ex's eyes widen, his hands lose their hold. He's flying backwards. Archie grabs the ex's throat with his left hand and spins him around so that the ex is now the one against the wall. He hoists Nadine's ex up against the wall until the ex's toes wobble against the littered, broken asphalt. Archie reaches for his Sig with his right hand. *Enough. I'm going to solve this problem the American way. My way.*

1722 HOURS

Chapter 18

"I T'S LOADED."

Archie opens his fingers. The ex collapses onto the ground and scrambles up and backwards. Using his Sig to point the direction of their mutual path, Archie backs the ex into the space between bins further down the alley. The bins hide them from the people on the street as well as anyone strolling in the alley that crosses the one they're in, and curious voyeurs peeking from windows and doors. Archie adjusts his hold on his grip and eases his finger from alongside the trigger guard toward the trigger. The ex freezes; his hands creep up into the air.

Ping.

Archie blinks.

His iPhone.

"Don't move," he warns the ex as he shifts the pistol from his right hand to his left in order to retrieve his iPhone from his inside pocket. "I'm ambidextrous."

The ex doesn't move.

Archie flicks on his iPhone, raising it to the same level as the ex's face so that he can watch both the ex and read the screen. Archie's forefinger remains alongside the trigger guard as he presses down the Home button. His iPhone vibrates in obedience. "Read messages," Archie tells Siri. Siri reads out loud the one new message in her chirpy artificial voice after saying who it's from and when it was sent. Hearing who the sender is blanks Archie's mind. Ma. Archie isn't sure what to make of her messaging him. Ma's words repeat in his head like rhythmic hammer blows: "Thank you, thank you for serving, my son. I hope you are well. We miss you. Come back soon."

Ma, who hasn't messaged or emailed him since he left for Canada. Sir had told his retreating back: "Your Mom isn't going to talk to you for this. You're leaving her, and I'll have to pick up the pieces from this. You're breaking your Mom's heart, you know."

Archie had felt nothing. Ma was the silent type, hardly said a word, simply cooked and looked after them all. Archie cannot recall having a conversation with her that lasted longer than two minutes. He repeats the message silently to himself. He notices she omitted, "I love you." Or "Love Ma."

The ex stirs, trying to blend into the wall. Archie's forefinger shifts into trigger position while his hand holding the iPhone remains frozen in its upraised position. The ex's eyes widen in terror.

Swoosh.

"Read the email," Archie commands Siri.

Siri tells him who it's from. She reads out loud the subject line: "Happy Veteran's Day."

Happy? Archie wonders morosely. *Who considers Veterans Day a happy occasion? Greeting card companies.* And then the name of the sender drops into his consciousness: his father's name. Curiosity and grief get the better of him, and he unlocks his iPhone to read the email.

It's a gif. There are fireworks exploding behind an elephant in Arctic camouflage, saluting him. "Happy Veteran's Day!" it reads.

"Thank you for serving your country. You've done your time. You've protected us. You've made us proud." Underneath the gif, Sir had typed a few words: "It was a righteous shoot. I hope you be happy, son."

A can rolling over a heaved crack in the asphalt focuses Archie's eyes back onto Nadine's ex and solidifies his left arm into shooting position. The ex squeaks: "It wasn't me. I'm not moving, man."

Swoosh.

Archie narrows his eyes at him. He slides his eyes to read the new email while holding the ex in his sensory view. The email is a picture, this time of the stars and stripes flying in the wind of war. "Thank you, thank you, thank you," is written all over the flag. Stephen had written underneath it: "I hope you have a great day bro."

Bro?

Who's Stephen hanging out with that he needs to impress? Did one of his marks find out about his twin serving in the army and make some innocent remark about remembering him on Veterans' Day? I can hear the conversation now. A scowl deepens the lines on either side of Archie's mouth, grooves canyons between his eyes, and blackens his deep-brown eyes. The imagined conversation grips his mind: "You got a brother in the army? He's a vet? You must be so proud. I bet he got a medal, too? He did? You served with him? No? But I bet you remembered what he did for all of us. You must be proud of him. I'm proud of all the soldiers who serve our great country. What'd you do for Veterans Day, send him an e-card?" And Stephen would've said. "Yes," and then sent him the e-card to show his client he had. Some things Stephen didn't fudge the truth about. One of them was over veterans. And he, Archie, was a veteran.

He glances at the ex. The ex's face is white, whiter than his eyes. His arms stretch high into the air; the backs of his hands flat against the blackened-red brick wall behind him with its shards of peeling paint left from some decades-old paint job. Archie stares at him, and the ex doesn't blink. He's holding his breath, and his eyes shake in their sockets as he runs out of air but doesn't dare breathe any fresh air in.

Ping.

"Damn it!" Archie spits out and looks at his iPhone's screen.

Squeak.

Archie snaps his eyes back onto the ex. The ex's eyelids drop to half staff; he freezes under Archie's brown-eyed glare. The ex quivers. His rolls of fat shake like jelly; his mouth gulps fish like; but his vocal cords have seized up after their unintended emittance. He cannot speak nor defend himself.

Archie makes a moue of disgust. Archie shifts his forefinger back to lie alongside the trigger guard and readies his arm to shoot. He doesn't want to inadvertently shoot jelly, but the ex isn't getting the message. He shifts his gaze back to his iPhone. A rustle jerks his attention back to the ex's white face. The ex is breathing again. "Turn around," Archie snarls. The ex's head wobbles. Archie imperceptibly stiffens his back into a steel shaft. His forefinger drifts back over the trigger, his head still and strong on top of his muscular neck. "Turn. Around." The ex turns around.

"Put your hands against the wall." The ex flattens his palms against the wall. His body trembles.

"Spread your legs apart." The ex obeys.

"Wider." The ex moves one leg further to the right. Then, under the silent force of Archie's eyes on his back, moves his left leg further to the left. His legs shake so hard, his knees are in danger of buckling.

"I don't hesitate to shoot," Archie growls. He waits a beat. "My pistol is aimed at your heart. Understood?" No answer. "Understood?!"

"Yes," the ex breathes back.

Archie commands Siri to read him the message while keeping his gaze locked on his target. Siri reads a message from Sally. When he hears Siri pronounce his wife's name, his heart constricts with gladness. Siri chirps: "Hey Archie. It's Veterans' Day. I hope y'all are having a great day up in Canada, wherever it is. I bet you got some parka on or something. I hear you live in igloos. Well, I have to go. Me and the girls are going shopping. They have great sales on for us today. Do you get Veterans sales up there? I guess not with living in the snow and all. I hope you got peace up there. I forgive you." Archie grins. He'd left her, yet she'd remembered him.

His family remembers him.

All of them.

At once.

They hadn't all remembered him on the same day since he'd come back from Afghanistan shortly before that first Veterans Day in Albuquerque.

They had held a welcoming party for him, his family, their friends, neighbours, and Stephen's clients. Balloons had stood straight at attention from every branch and pole outside his parents' home. Sally had moved in with his parents while he'd been fighting in Afghanistan. She didn't want to live on base in another state, so far from her friends. He'd applauded her move. He'd shared all the secrets of the house, and they'd laughed over his parents' quirks, Ma's propensity to say not one word during breakfast while she cooked them all heuvos rancheros and only three words during lunch: "Come to the table." "Four words," Sally had corrected him in their first Skype after having emailed each other for the first few weeks when he'd been stationed with the 5th Combat Brigade Team. He'd been careful to tell her nothing about his experiences with the team. And when they'd begun Skyping, he'd wash his face and hands and slip on his one clean shirt he kept in his sack for just that purpose— for talking to Sally, Ma and Sir, and his twin Stephen so that they'd never know the hellhole he was in.

Sally had done up their bedroom in pretty laces and linen. She'd gotten a brand new nightie for herself, and risque underwear, so that when he undressed her piece by piece, all her prettiness would be on display. She'd gotten a fresh dye job, and her blonde highlights gleamed under the New Mexico sun when he'd first seen her standing there, waiting for him by Sir's car. Her hair had gleamed and her face had shone in the candlelight of their bedroom. His parents and Stephen had left the house when Sally had pulled him by the hand into their bedroom. Having dared to dream of this moment in the days leading up to returning, he'd found himself feeling unsure. Taking off her clothes had felt foreign to him. Sand and rocks and the hardness of guns and ammo were what his hands were used to. The bump of his ass on the hard driver's seat, worn down from continual jostling during hours of driving, and grinding of gears and straining engines, were his experiences for what had seemed like his entire life. The pungency of burning oil and burning batteries and burning metal still seared his nostrils, and Sally's floral perfume had irritated his nose. The powdery scent had seemed to mock his memory of the sweet smell of blood in desert heat.

He never wanted to smell again.

Sally had not taken his rejection well when his hands had frozen midway through slipping her dress off when he'd seen her pretty pink bra and briefs in lacy polyester decorated with feminine-pink rosettes. How could he touch something so delicate with his dirty and grubby and hardened soul? He'd only stain her with his horror. Like a tsunami, fatigue had washed over him, and he'd collapsed into bed for his last long, dreamless sleep.

The next morning, he'd arrived at the breakfast table, with his entire family waiting to greet him. Sally had followed him more slowly, acting all flushed and awkward as if they'd had a passionate night. She'd fallen languidly into her chair and fanned her face at how hot it was. He'd sat down expressionless. Ma had placed a plate of stacked flapjacks in front of him. He'd frowned and looked up at her. "Special," she'd said and turned back to her stove. He'd looked back down at his plate, hoping to see the familiar heuvos rancheros with red and green chile sauce. Chile red, chile green smothering the white of egg and caramelized-splotched-brown tortilla underneath, not the fluffy pale blonde of flapjacks. The flapjacks reminded him of the day of his righteous shoot. Maybe it was their desert-blonde colour. Ma rarely cooked flapjacks and never till their edges browned to crispness. She slipped them pale off the griddle. Or maybe it was the height of the flapjack stack that had set his memories twitching. They'd leaned at a crazy angle like a man about to fall down. Staring at that stack, Archie's chest had constricted, and he'd emptied into their flowing conversation the memory of his righteous shoot. Sir had clapped him on the back at how he could never hear that story enough times and at how bravely he'd protected them all. Stephen had chortled at how the Tal-i-ban who'd been gunning for him must've looked when he got beat by Archie. "Bet he didn't see that coming, brother!" he'd crowed while bile rose in Archie's throat and horror turned his eyes into staring orbs. Ma had slipped heuvos rancheros next to his flapjacks and served him a plateful of hash browns. She'd smacked Stephen's hand as he reached out to scoop some from his pile.

Archie had eaten his entire breakfast, including the flapjacks, trying to join in their revelry over shooting that "Tal-i-ban" dead. "He got what was coming to him!" the four had crowed. They didn't care it was a village man, not the Taliban; they saw no difference. They boasted how Archie knew how to shoot because he came from a state that knew what guns were for and didn't hold with no gun control like those northern states. "Your gun saved your life, your platoon's lives, Archie's. Never forget that," Sir had pointed his fork at him.

Archie's saved life became their saved lives, became America's saved existence. They'd celebrated the whole day. Ma had gathered the neighbours, and Sir had hosted a neighbourhood party where people had toasted Archie long into the small hours of the next day. He'd drunk Tequila that night. Tequila and beer made it all better.

But Sally didn't forgive him his rejection his first night home. She didn't forget he couldn't make love to her. Archie couldn't explain how the sight of her made him loathe himself. The army had discharged him on his return. Fortunately, his worker had gotten him diagnosed with PTSD and into counselling within weeks of returning. His VA counsellor had said this was normal, that Sally should come see him so that he could help them with their marriage. But Sally had told him her girlfriends thought he was just having man problems. "You have to figure out your own problems, Archie. I don't have no problems," she'd spat in his face and flounced away.

Her anger at his rejection, his drinking, his doubts over his righteous shoot had erupted into shouting at his silent visage over his drinking more and more beer every night. His drinking had stretched backwards in time from dinner into lunch. And that last day, when he was supposed to see his VA counsellor and had found him gone, that morning had been the first day he'd had beer for breakfast. His first liquid breakfast.

Ma had said nothing. Sir had joked he was taking this soldier thing too far. "When are you going to admit that Tal-i-ban deserved to be shot? Son, you didn't know he didn't have a gun. Empty hands don't mean shit. He could've been concealed carrying. You gotta watch out and assume everyone's carrying. That's how you stay alive."

The last Veterans Day in his home state, Archie had refused to attend the parade. Disgust had distorted Sir's features as he'd turned his back on Archie. Stephen had castigated him for jeopardizing some business deal he was working on. "What are my clients gonna think?" he'd yelled. "You're a coward, not patriotic enough, that's what they'll think! I can't have a brother who's not patriotic." He'd flicked his hand at Archie and stormed out. Archie had slammed shut his bedroom door so hard, the hinges had shifted. He'd glared at the listing door while he'd drunk himself stupid, loading and unloading Pawpaw's Outdoorsman. Archie can't recall what Ma had done that day or where Sally had gone to. He pounds his head, but the memories remain locked while eating his nerves from the depths of their hidden cave.

Ma, Sir, Sally, and Stephen had ignored him ever since he'd left for Canada. Guilt egging him when he'd landed at Pearson International Airport, he'd messaged them all that he'd arrived safely. He mailed them birthday cards on each of their birthdays because, with distance, the relationships seemed to him less and less fractured. They hadn't reciprocated. No birthday cards or Christmas cards for Archie. No emails. No messages. Until today.

Archie's heart implodes.

Grief blurs the iPhone screen, plunging him into a plummet-less pool, swamping his momentary happiness. Why now? Why on this day do they at last remember he exists? Why do they suddenly care? Who told them to acknowledge his existence, to pretend they give a fuck he lives? What guilt eats them? What do they want? Tears spill down his cheeks and clog his nose. Saliva thickens into a gooey mucus carpet on his tongue. *When I needed their attention, their kindness, their remembrance, all they gave me was lectures. Man up, son. Be a real husband. Be a patriot. Stop drinking.* A sob chokes his breath. *I did stop drinking. The day I set foot in Canada is the day I stopped. Canada changed everything.*

Andrew had taken him to a health food store and had shown him the vitamins, minerals, and supplements he needed to keep sane and healthy. Archie'd begun roaming the city with the map Andrew had given him. But after the second day out, he'd left the map in his rooming-house bedroom. He only wanted to wander. The walking had quietened his soul. He'd learnt to shut away the ache of missing. He'd berated himself: *your family left you, Specialist, long before you physically left them.*

Now they remember.

Now they care.

It's too late. Bitterness bites Archie's tongue.

How do you cope with what you've wanted when it comes years after you needed it and years after giving up ever seeing it? The years of suffering alone, of being told how to feel about the shoot, of being rejected for his doubts, his nightmares, his PTSD anxiety, suffuse his body with aches, coagulate his shoulders into boards of pain, pressurize his head until the force of his emotions pushes against his temples, threatening to explode his brain through his skull, scalp, and hair, compressing his teeth together into paroxysms of harsh pain that scrapes into his gums and overfills his sinuses. Fluid of grief swells every cell in his body, pushing outward against their containing walls.

Physical pain ratchets up. Years of loss flagellate the messages' heralding of change and overload his mind. He'd needed them years ago. Today, they show up. Today, they tantalize him with a taste of what could've been, of how his suffering could've been so much less. *If only they'd been kind, if only they'd accepted and supported me, if only they'd gone with me to my VA counsellor, if only they'd walked with me, sat with me like Pawpaw used to, if only they'd said, "Though we cannot understand what war's like, what you went through, only your peers can do that, we're here for you, we're here to hold you, to listen, and to be with you," if only they'd reached out a hand and had never let me go, never let me be alone to drown in my memories until the day I shot myself on the wrong side of the chest.*

Sally had walked in the house too early, chattering over her shoulder in her treble voice to her friend trailing and nodding behind her. Her sudden appearance had startled him, and his shaking, drunken hand had jerked sideways while his finger had pulled the trigger. The bang had ricocheted sound waves off the walls, the floor, the ceiling. Archie hadn't felt a thing. Sally had screamed: "Archie!" Her friend's mouth had opened slowly in a long oval, her eyes had raised heavenward, and she'd collapsed to the floor with flopping arms and legs, hitting it without a sound. He realized later the shot had deafened him to all sounds but Sally's screams. "Archie! How could you do that to me! I just met her! My first real friend! And you had to go and shoot yourself. How could you be so careless?!"

Archie had looked down to see the fabric of his shirt torn off. The bullet had torn a chunk out of his side and taken a shard of rib with it. In shock, he'd looked back up at Sally, her voice having gone unhearable while her mouth kept moving like a machine gun belt feeding bullets. At the VA hospital, doctors had stitched the wound closed and then sent the paperwork to the VA counsellor. Contemplating the gauze still protecting his stitched-up shot side, the counsellor had asked him what had happened. Relief had sagged Archie that somebody was again listening to him.

Archie relaxes under that remembered empathy; then the shame of what he'd done burns his stomach anew. His VA counsellor had spoken of hope in subsequent visits but not his suicide attempt. His father Sir had told him he was out of practice in cleaning his gun, that that was what had happened. Sir had ordered Archie to stop talking about it as if it was not accidental. Sally had told him never to speak of it and berated him for losing her a good friend. Ma had gazed upon him with sad eyes and mute mouth. And Stephen had avoided him for three months until he felt he was safe from hearing about that subject.

Archie had learnt to keep his mouth shut. Suicide was not a topic even professionals wanted to talk about. His VA counsellor hadn't wanted to hear Archie speak out loud his terrible thoughts of self-harm, only the good things he was doing in the present. "Keep your thoughts focused on the positive," he'd instructed him every session.

They had all shut him out.

His eyes refocus on the black screen of his iPhone. He presses the Home button, and his lock screen shines into the alley's shadowed light. His thumb unlocks the iPhone, and he reads the last message again. The light of their reaching out deepens the rejection that had dug a chasm between them and him. Their rejection and judgement, their abandoning him to his VA counsellor to deal with his sickness—"You're sick, son, when is that VA counsellor going to make you right, make you see what you done was good?" The chasm, with its churning river of accusations and its steep walls of demands to be healthy, cannot be filled in with a few messages shot through cyberspace.

Archie's emotions flee.

His tanned face resumes its accustomed mask of neutrality and power.

His thumb presses down the iPhone's Power button.

Click.

Archie refocuses on the ex's sagging back as he slips the iPhone back into its pocket. Archie assesses his target with vacant eyes. He lifts his right hand to cradle the Sig's grip in both hands. He lifts his chest up higher against the pain that strains to bend him. He stretches his neck from one shoulder to the other, the muscle fibres cracking all along his neck, first one side then the other, while he keeps his eyes dead on the surrendering back before him. Archie deliberately shifts the pistol into a right-handed grip and places his right forefinger into the trigger position.

Time to end this.

1800 HOURS

Chapter 19

"Hey!" The shout from the end of the alley veers Archie's attention from his target to the shout's source. He senses a lunge; he kicks toward his target without seeing him. Archie hears a whoosh, a dull floppy thud, and a sigh of helplessness. Out of the corner of his left eye, he glances towards his target flopped against the bricks as he peeks around the bin and, with his main vision, trains his focus on the alley's mouth. Two figures. Shades against the glare of the street.

Archie steps back towards the wall and looks down at his deflated target. He curls his lip and growls: "Get up."

The ex sobs. He raises his hands up to his face, his shoulders shaking, his body curling in towards the dirty crack between bricks and asphalt. He lifts his head, and his face stained with tears, he cries: "Why?"

"Hey Archie, are you there?" Andrew's voice floats down the alley towards Archie. He stills himself and raises a finger to his closed lips. The ex gulps in his tears.

"Archie?" Andrew draws closer. His footsteps echo in another pair of footsteps as he marches down the alley. The ex's tears dry; his eyes brighten with anger; redness crawls through his cheeks along the blue lines of his veins. He stands up shakily, clenching his fists and lowering his head like a bull. Archie trains his pistol on his target's forehead and whispers: "I don't miss." The ex's eyes dart to behind Archie's right shoulder. He smiles cunningly and raises his arms, fists extended. His legs straighten.

"There you are, Archie," Andrew says in an easy voice. Archie doesn't turn around, doesn't move his eyes. He remains trained on his target, the threat that won't leave him alone.

"Leave," Archie commands in a low tone. "This is not your concern."

"You are my concern, Archie," Andrew replies. Archie hears him shift his booted feet apart into the familiar "at ease" stance. Archie tightens his grip on his Sig. He watches his target's eyes dart from himself to Andrew, hears the target speak: "He started it."

Archie feels a whisper of air behind him as Andrew says: "It looks like something is going on here. Tell me what happened, Archie."

"Him!" Archie feels his target's shout shoot food-fouled air across his right cheek. "Why you asking him? He's got the gun. Can't you tell he's the one started it!"

Andrew replies, "Yes, I see that. It's a Sig Sauer P320, isn't it Archie?"

"Why you talking to him!"

Archie shifts his weight and begins to squeeze the trigger. It's a familiar effortful pull. He knows how much pressure to apply and when to anticipate the bullet leaving its chamber, to speed through the thin black muzzle hidden in the shaft of nickel steel, to smash air molecules apart and the sound barrier, and to explode the head of his target. Archie tires of waiting. He wants this to end, and to end now. He's tired of feeling. He wants all feelings to end, and to end now. He no longer wants to think, to remember. He wants thoughts and memories to end, and to end now. Andrew's words glide into his consciousness. "He has the pistol, and I believe he's about to shoot."

Archie sees his target's eyes widen in concert with his mouth opening into a round circle, revealing his nicotine-stained teeth. What did Nadine ever see in the target? He'll be doing the world a favour by eliminating this threat.

"Ridding the world of this man won't solve the problem, Specialist."

Archie blinks and stops exerting pressure on the trigger. His shoulders relax infinitesimally.

"Can we talk about it, Specialist?"

Archie says nothing and refocuses on his target. His shoulders reposition to support his arms holding the gun.

Andrew calmly continues: "It won't take long. Talking doesn't have to take long, and you can still shoot him." Archie hears a squeak but listens to Andrew. "I'd like to understand first what's going on. I am the commanding officer here."

Archie draws his brows together, trying to follow Andrew but not wanting to lose sight of his target down the barrel of his pistol. The target is situated at the white point between the back two white points of his pistol's night sight. He can train his pistol clearly on the target in the gloom of this alley.

The target won't shut up: "He still has his gun on me! You're not doing anything!"

Archie relaxes his brows. He knows what to do and begins exerting slow, steady pressure on the trigger again. In his right peripheral vision, Archie sees Andrew raise his right hand in a relaxed gesture, palm out towards his target. Archie doesn't stop.

Andrew says: "I'd like to talk, Specialist, about this threat. Can we talk first?"

Archie willfully switches his entire focus to the threat. Andrew raises the volume of his voice but keeps his tone calm. "Specialist, I'm not familiar with this threat. Explain him to me."

Against his will, Archie obeys Andrew. He stops squeezing the trigger and replies: "Yes, sir. He's my target."

"Who's your target?"

Archie blinks.

"Who is this man?"

"Man?"

"Yes. I want to understand. Who is this man? You can tell me, Specialist."

Archie swallows as he stares at the face of his target that slowly changes into an identity. Nadine's Ex. He speaks it.

"I remember you were concerned about him. Tell me more."

"He believes we had an affair. He is pursuing me."

"I see. Why is he pursuing you, Specialist?"

Salty moisture drips into Archie's eyes. Archie shakes his head to clear his vision. His target charges him, and Archie squeezes the trigger fully. The bullet fires past his target's face, scoring a blood trail along his cheek, and enters the brick wall. The target screams, clamps his hand against his left cheek, and jumps backwards. Blood oozes through the cracks between his fingers. His jaw drops, but no sound comes out anymore from him.

Archie says in a bloodless voice: "Missed." Anger seeps in. "I don't miss. Ever."

Andrew replies as Archie quickly returns to shooting position: "No, you don't miss, Specialist. Let's talk about that."

"What's there to talk about."

"About why you missed. The threat is immobilized."

"He's standing, sir."

"Yes, he is, Specialist. But he's not moving."

Archie scans the human mass in the sight of his Sig while listening to the whispers of litter skittering along the asphalt, the far-off hum of traffic, his commanding officer's even breathing, a shout of laughter and answering voices moving past the alley mouth. Andrew is correct. The target is frozen in a caricature of The Scream, the only movement, fresh blood flowing bright-red ribbons over his fingers. Crimsoning drops hover in ever lengthening gooey strands from his pinky finger before they release themselves and plummet to the ground. Archie follows the drops' paths briefly and notices how worn the target's sneakers are.

Andrew's voice breaks into Archie's surveillance. "Who is this man, Archie?"

Archie assesses the sneakers. Worn, scuffed, unkempt, lazy. Cheesy foot odour separates from rotting meat, wet boxes, and rain-washed asphalt. He lifts his eyes back quickly to the man's face. The Scream remains suspended in time. The Scream transforms in his perception into familiar features. His commanding officer waits, his breathing even, his stance unhurried. Archie processes the features and his internal assessment of the sneakers. The Scream is Nadine's ex. Those are the shoes of Nadine's ex. He's beaten the ex before. He can do so again.

Archie nods inside himself.

It's safe for him to talk. For a minute. The pounding rhythm of must end, must end, must end, my story must end, isn't lessening. How long can he hold himself against it?

Andrew asks: "Can we talk, Specialist? Tell me what happened."

Archie says: "He came after me again, sir."

"What did he do, Specialist?"

"He threw me into this alley, sir."

"I see. He caught you off guard." Andrew states it flatly, calmly.

Archie hears judgement. "I apologize, sir."

Andrew replies: "Nothing to apologize for, Specialist. It's a busy city. The best cannot always distinguish threats from friends."

"Yes, sir." Archie's self-flagellation underlies his obedient tone.

Andrew says: "Even though he caught you by surprise, you got the upper hand, didn't you?"

Archie cocks his head. Andrew waits. "Yes, sir, I did, sir."

"I'd expect no less from you, Specialist. You're well trained."

"Yes, sir. Thank you, sir."

"We all get surprised, Specialist, but it's what you do afterwards that counts. And you came through."

"Yes, sir."

"You isolated the threat so that he couldn't harm anyone. You've protected the public and Nadine, Specialist."

Archie says with birthing confidence and thought. "Yes, sir."

"You isolated him to protect the public. You took control, Specialist."

"I did, sir." Archie shifts his position so that he can see Andrew a little easier while maintaining eyes on the ex, a blobby, contained threat. Andrew's face is open. No judgement lurks in it. No lie. Behind Andrew, Archie recognizes the second shade. David is standing down the alley, arms hanging loose, hands relaxed. David's entire stance is like that of a man watching dogs playing in a park. Archie returns his attention to Andrew and the ex.

"Now that you've isolated him, we have time, don't we, Specialist?"

"I don't know, sir."

"Look around you, you've done well. No one is at risk here, isn't that right, Specialist?"

Archie steals a look beyond Andrew; he carefully turns his head to survey the other direction while keeping his senses alert for any movement. "Correct, sir."

"We have more than a minute to talk, then, Specialist?"

Archie admits reluctantly: "I guess so, sir."

"Good," Andrew says positively, putting calmness, praise, and good feelings into that word as much as he can. His energy flows into Archie. A thought eases into Archie's head that maybe he can spare a few minutes more. Maybe there's no rush. The thought struggles against the onslaught of must end, must end, must end emanating from deep inside him, but the thought prevails.

Andrew says: "So let's talk about that control, Specialist. Can we do that?"

"Yes, sir," Archie replies, latching on to Andrew's words, being held by Andrew's unthreatening blue eyes. He adds: "I want to eliminate the threat, sir." Archie yearns for approval from his commanding officer.

"Why?" Andrew asks with simple curiosity.

Archie frowns in confusion at the unexpected question. No thoughts come. Yet the thudding thought, must end, must end, must end, he and the threat must go, doesn't let up. It gallops around and around and around in his head.

"Why, Specialist, tell me why you want to eliminate the threat."

Archie stares with confusion at the crimson-stained face before him. "He's a threat, sir."

Andrew raises his right arm, palm outward, toward the threat. "Nadine's ex is no threat, Specialist. He's frozen and can't harm anyone."

Archie shakes his head. "That's not true, sir. He's pursued me three times today."

"I see. Tell me about the first time."

Archie shakes his head.

Andrew asks him again: "Tell me about the first time, Specialist. Help me understand the sequence of events."

Archie says nothing.

"You know how we plan a successful assault, Specialist? The commanding officer must have all the facts in order to assess the situation and strategize the attack. Correct, Specialist?"

"Correct, sir."

"Tell me about the first time."

Archie does. In a detached voice, he tells the brick wall how the ex had found him and banged on his door and how he'd gotten rid of him.

Andrew praises him. "You executed your plan well, Specialist. You got rid of the threat and protected your men in the rooming house. Good job, Specialist."

Archie swells with pride, and his face relaxes a mite. Andrew builds on that. "Tell me about the second time."

Archie does, and as he does, he moves his primary focus from the ex to Andrew's open face.

Andrew nods his head in approval. "Good job, Specialist, good job," Andrew effuses, his blue eyes smiling and relaxed. Archie lifts the edges of his lips in return. His torso relaxes, and he drops his arms a little.

But then a movement. Archie's face hardens. His eyes lock back on the ex. "But he's still here, sir. I haven't eliminated him."

"That's true, Specialist," Andrew replies. "Let's talk about how to eliminate him without harming you."

"Why, sir?"

"Because we, David, Nadine, and I, don't want to see you harmed, Archie."

Archie blinks as sweat rolls into his eyes. Pools of moisture expand under his arms and along the length of his belt encircling his waist. He shakes the salty drops out of his eyes; he eases his legs further apart and lifts his shoulders up to his ears and relaxes them back into position. The sweat, though, won't stop spurting from his skin.

Sunlight shafts into the alley, lighting up the brick wall and the man standing frozen before him. Bird song penetrates his hearing. Insistent chirps of happiness fill the air above him. Cars hiss along the street at the end of the alley. A loose manhole cover clank-clanks as a car drives over it.

Andrew repeats: "We don't want to see you harmed, Archie. You're a good soldier. We need good soldiers."

"I'm not," Archie growls.

"What makes you say that? You were an asset to our team in Afghanistan. You guarded our backs while we negotiated with the village elders. You learnt our strengths and taught us your US-honed skills. We welcomed you to Canada because we like you and respect you. You are part of us, and we you."

"Remember when I got us stuck, and you were the one…"

"We all have that happen to us. Mistakes happen no matter how well trained. It's what you do afterwards to make things right that matters. What happened in your Combat Team went against what you stood for and who we fought for. You stood up for what was right against men who pulled out all the stops to make you believe their hate and fear was the best way. You're an honest soldier. We were glad to have you join our platoon as a Specialist from the US Army. You were and are an asset to our team. We can't afford to lose you. We don't want to lose you."

Archie quakes. His brow wrinkles; his face contorts. Time to end this vies with the desire to give over to another.

"It's time to give me the pistol, Specialist. I will take over."

Archie looks over at Andrew. The idea of handing responsibility to him appeals to Archie. He doesn't want to die. He simply wants it to end.

"No one has to die today, Specialist." Andrew says in a soft voice. "Not you, not him. I will handle this for you, Archie, just give me the pistol."

Weariness and relief crash into each other and splash up into Archie's mind. They clear his eyes, and he sees the ex is just a pathetic man. He nods and drops his arms. Andrew throws a warning glance toward Nadine's ex. But the ex has learnt his lesson and doesn't twitch. Archie continues to hold his Sig in his right hand, but his forefinger is no longer on the trigger but lying alongside the trigger guard. Archie stares at the ground.

"Specialist, give me the pistol." Andrew holds out his right hand, palm up, fingers open. Archie lifts his eyes from the fractured asphalt to Andrew's relaxed face and firm eyes. Archie doesn't want to die, but he doesn't want to give up the option. He can trust Andrew; if Andrew says he will take care of the ex, then he will. But he cannot give up his combat pistol. A man must always have an option. Swiftly, Archie holsters his Sig in his concealed carry, skirts around Andrew, and strides down the alley towards the street. David steps in front of him; Archie halts; Andrew says loudly but calmly, "Let him go, David. He's safe when there's no threat."

David eyes Archie. Archie returns his stare impassively, the need to escape scratching at him but not breaking his expressionlessness. David shakes his head but steps to the side. Archie resumes striding to the street. Archie hears the ex yelling: "Are you going to let him go like that?" And Andrew's firm voice replying: "He won't harm you now. I told him I'm taking care of you, and I will. Let's talk about this."

"Talk? Are you crazy? You need to lock him up."

"Let's talk about what happened here first. Tell me about Nadine and your breakup."

"She broke up with me. It has to be his fault!"

As Archie exits the alley and enters the blaring street, Archie last hears Andrew asking in his calm, commanding voice: "Tell me about it, about your breakup, about today." And the ex's reply: "Okay. I will if that will get you to go after him faster! She—."

1900 HOURS

Chapter
20

Archie parades along, his long legs eating up the kilometres, his body knifing skillfully between people crowding the narrow sidewalk, strolling, talking, hurrying, milling. Sanity seeps back into his mind. No way I could've gotten away with a homicide in Toronto, he admits. Andrew had informed him in his first month here when he'd spotted his guns in his bedroom that the Toronto Police Service has an excellent arrest rate for homicides. It'd been a mild statement, but Andrew's intent had been clear. Toronto doesn't tolerate gun shootings or gun deaths. There will be no righteous shoots here in Canada. Relief had flooded Archie at hearing that. Reality resides here. A death is a death; killing is killing. Call it what it is. Don't sugarcoat it. It was like that when he'd told his Canadian platoon about his grandfather's—

Archie shudders, interrupting his marching flow. Suicide. One of them...Archie frowns. Which one? Archie's brow clears as he remembers. Nadine! She'd uttered the S-word unflinchingly. Suicide. That's all she'd said. Everything was in that one word:

sympathy, empathy with him over his loss, sadness that Pawpaw had chosen that way, understanding for his reasons, and sorrow he couldn't see the outreached hand to healing. Archie halts as the traffic light in front of him turns amber. There is something in his thoughts he should pay attention to. Archie bows his head and frowns at the sidewalk's drying concrete. He struggles to remember what he was thinking; tries to recall the word that had triggered a thought. But both are lost to him.

Archie shudders. He lifts his head to watch the red light as people gather around him, waiting for the walk sign to turn to a white man walking.

The cross traffic clears, but their light remains red. That doesn't deter a couple of men in business suits and a woman in leg-hugging black stretchy pants, bright yellow sneakers, and several layers of pink and blue long-sleeved tops. They cross against the red. Archie waits. He doesn't want to draw attention to himself, not even for jay walking.

Ping. His iPhone notifies him a message has arrived.

The light turns green at the same time as the red hand disappears and the white man walking appears.

Archie remains at the corner as he unlocks his iPhone and flips to the Signal app. Impatient Torontonians swirl around him. It's David.

"Yeah, so Andrew is talking to that ex of Nadine's. What's his name?"

Archie types quickly, his thumbs a blur: "Don't know." He shuts off his iPhone and retrains his eyes on the other side. But the countdown timer has begun already. Police consider it the same as the red hand. So he won't risk it, although he can cross the intersection easily in the seconds left. A plume of impatience stirs his feet. But his training takes over. *Wait, soldier,* he instructs himself. *Good things come to those who wait.* Archie had learnt how to wait, how to stand in one place watching for threats, waiting for a command. He can wait forty seconds for a light change.

Archie blinks rapidly as he thinks about where he is. He's down on the Lakeshore. He's not sure how he got to this place where multi-lanes of traffic wait huffily at their lines underneath the downtown highway and the traffic lights favour them speeding east-west across the southern edge of the city. The concrete ribbons above trap the exhaust billowing from cars and trucks below. Maybe two minutes he'll have to wait.

Ping.

With a sigh, he unbuttons his jacket again and reaches in for his iPhone. Archie reads David's next message. "We don't know either, and Andrew doesn't want to piss him off asking. I texted Nadine, but she's not answering. She's in the shower or something. The sergeant can't get clean enough. Ever since Afghanistan, she takes like 5 or 6 showers a day."

Archie reads that and doesn't know what to say. He returns his iPhone to its accustomed pocket and buttons up one button on his jacket. His fingers pause in their upward motion to the next button as he ponders, *David will probably message me again. He's in a chatty mood. And when David gets messaging, he won't stop till he's done.* Archie deflates. David doesn't care whether or not his platoon buddies want to talk. He's there for them, so be there for me, is David's stance.

Archie sweeps resentment out of his head. It's only right. That's why we're here: for each other. His blown-up friend's teaching of Jesus's friendship during their prayer services and his counsellor's words that relationships take work, echo in his head. He came here seeking a home, people who understood him, who didn't judge but wanted to know him, talk to him, hear his story, banter and spend time with him, in all his ugly emotions and reviled thinking. They haven't swerved once from him. Unlike his family. Archie manipulates the button out of its buttonhole as his light turns green again and hunts around in all his pockets for his iPhone earbuds. His fingertips feel the rubbery coil in the right-hand inner pocket of his dress uniform jacket. He pulls out the earbuds, retrieves his iPhone from his jacket's left-hand inner pocket, plugs the earbuds into his iPhone, pushes the buds into his ears, and slides his iPhone back into its place. He buttons up both jackets, settles his shoulders down, and marches across the intersection, both arms swinging in tune with his legs.

Ping.

The artificial sound jabs both eardrums.

Archie grimaces. He snatches the right cord leading from the right earbud and presses the lower part of the earbuds' volume rocker several times. He then depresses the middle part of the rocker until he hears Siri's chime. He tells her to read his message. She does. And so it goes. He walks in steady time. Siri reads David's messages into his ears, and Siri sends back his dictated replies.

David writes: "This guy is stuck on you having an affair with Nadine. What'd you do?"

"Nothing."

"C'mon man, You musta done something."

"She's my sergeant."

"She's more than that. We're all buddies."

"Yes."

"Did you hang with her when we weren't around?"

Archie is about to say no when his feet slow down. A memory tickles his mind. There was that one time. "We met for coffee at Starbucks that one time when she was having trouble finding a job. I let her vent."

"OK, OK. That must be it. I'll tell Andrew."

Archie walks two more blocks before another message from David pings. "That was it. This guy thinks cause you met at Starbucks and Nadine didn't tell him, you must be having an affair."

"OK."

"He's crying. Geeze, he's sobbing like a baby."

Archie thinks about all the times the men had sobbed on each other's shoulders when back at base after terrible days or out in the field in the privacy of their tents. He thinks about the times David has taken his messages late at night, knowing he was probably crying. It's okay to cry with your buddies. But if anyone not your buddy saw you cry...Archie quirks his mouth and shrugs. He recalls how Andrew had treated him earlier that day, how his compassion had calmed him. Andrew is good to everyone. He feels responsible for everyone. *Why should I resent him taking care of this guy, too? I shot him, and Andrew saved me from a homicide charge. He let me keep my pistol. Andrew trusts me.* Archie's feet stall in their rhythm. He restarts as he thinks, *Now Andrew's trying to keep the ex from bothering me again. If that means the ex cries...*Archie tells Siri to reply. "He's allowed to cry."

"Yeah, you're right. He's a civvie, and he's bothering you and Nadine. But I guess he's human too. We treated those men over there better than we treat our own civvies. I'll give you that."

Archie isn't sure what David means but leaves it. He carries on in his parade stride, passing by new landmarks. He doesn't recognize his surroundings, but the lake is to his south. *This city has this giant body of water to orient yourself to,* he marvels. *Even when lost, you just find that water and know which way to head.*

Ping.

"Andrew is listening to him. He's got his hand on the guy's shoulder. The ex is sobbing about how Nadine doesn't love him. I wouldn't love him either."

Archie snorts. "I wouldn't either. But then I'm not a girl."

"LOLOLOL!"

Archie lengthens his stride. He quickens his rhythm.

"Andrew's talking to the guy quietly. I can't hear much, wondering if I can creep closer so I can hear. It's like we were taught how to walk quietly."

A couple of minutes tick their seconds off.

Ping.

"I'm closer. The guy's looking at the ground, didn't hear me. Andrew's telling him Nadine's never had a boyfriend for very long. They all knew she'd leave him but not because he's a bad guy but that's just the way she is. The guy is sniffing. He seems to be buying it. Andrew's good."

Archie reflects on Nadine and her relationships in the time he's known her. Andrew's correct. The longest one lasted six months. He messages back: "Andrew's correct."

"Hey! You're right. I hadn't thought too much about how long she keeps a guy around. They never seemed serious, so's why should I pay attention? I put it down to her being picky."

Archie wonders, but a commotion boils up in front of him, drawing his attention away from the messaging conversation. A pedestrian is yelling at a cyclist. The cyclist is straddling his angled bike with one foot on the ground and the other on his pedal while informing the gesticulating pedestrian he has a right to bike there because cars are dangerous. The pedestrian shakes a fist. A woman stops to watch. A couple of men slow to gawk as they walk past. When the cyclist yells at the pedestrian, "I have a right to bike where I want," the three draw in close. Other pedestrians join the small and growing group. One of them shouts: "No, you don't. Pedestrians have the ultimate right in this city."

"You got that right. You get off the sidewalk!" echoes another.

"Or else what?" The cyclist sneers, oblivious to the fact his presumed rights are up against a forming mob. Archie shakes his head at the man's hubris. He adjusts his course to leave the altercation behind. He asks Siri to read him David's last messages to him.

"Andrew's told him Nadine likes him, but she's her own woman. You can't make someone love you. It's tough, but there it is."

"He's whining now. Why doesn't she love him. Andrew's pouring it on. She came back from Afghanistan. She can't handle relationships. She wants a man in her life but doesn't know how to get close."

"He's saying he can help her."

"No one can help her in that way. She has to heal. She's seeing a psychologist. The shrink—are psychologists shrinks?"

Archie doesn't think so and messages back, "No."

"Yeah, well, Andrew's telling him that her shrink said she can't handle relationships right now and needs to take a break. So's if anyone's at fault it's the doc."

Archie nods to no one. Makes sense to him. He couldn't relate to Sally. He was so afraid of hurting her just by being present, of his memories contaminating her beauty, her civilian innocence, he couldn't stand to be close to Sally. They should've taken a break.

"The guy's nodding. I think he's buying it. Andrew's asking him to keep away from you. The guy's saying" David had pressed Send before finishing the message.

Archie waits to hear what the ex said. A few minutes later David messages: "He's agreed you and Nadine didn't have an affair. He wants to apologize to Nadine. Andrew's convinced him not to approach you or go to the police because he assaulted you first. He gets it wouldn't be good for him either. He's real calm and resigned like. I don't think he'll come after you again. You're safe, man."

Archie stops his march so suddenly, his shoulders and head lurch forward, and he almost overbalances. Strength flees his thighs. He reaches out to hunt for the nearest wall. He collapses against it, his left shoulder taking the impact. His heart thuds, and his lungs noisily snatch for air. He hadn't realized how wound up with anxiety he was until now. He turns to face the street, keeping contact with the wall's cold hardness. His back to the wall, he centres his vision on the passing scene, and with a cleansing inhalation, he peddles his heels backward until he stretches his entire self from the back of his head to his heels up against the concrete brace. With his abdominal muscles, Archie yanks himself away from the temporary crutch. He strolls on.

Ping.

"The guy wants to apologize to Nadine. Andrew's trying to get him to wait on that. He's nodding his head, but I don't think he's going to wait. He's told Andrew to apologize to you from him. No way he's going near you again. Andrew's convinced him. Can't believe Andrew had to spend 4 minutes convincing him of that after you shot him!"

Archie can't believe it either. Nadine's ex is stupid. What did she ever see in him? Archie's relieved Andrew's words worked and they're more powerful than his pistol and his hands.

"OK, we're good. The ex has gone. And we're headed home."

"OK," Archie messages back. The day is almost done. It's winding down better than he had hoped. No one is dead today.

2000 HOURS

Chapter
21

ARCHIE'S IPHONE BUZZES in his pocket: three long, two short vibrations. Repeated. It's his Do Not Disturb hour; he'd switched off his ringer a second before at 2000 hours. But the vibrations persist. Reluctantly, he extracts his iPhone from his pocket and unlocks it with his forefinger. Misgiving burbles in him at Nadine's rare use of iMessage. His thumb hovers over the iMessage app. With a sudden downward thrust, he launches the app and sees Nadine's name again. His mind hesitates as his thumb quickly presses on her name to read her message. It's a long one, and it begins with an "I'm sorry."

Archie's heart rat-a-tat-tat-tats. Blood swells his arteries in his ears and pounds in concert with the rapid-fire beats in his chest. He doesn't want to read. He reads:

"I'm sorry, guys. I shot him. There, I wrote it, my secret. I had to out it. It was best to put his suffering down. I won't be court-martialled for it. It's Man-Love Thursday, and he pleaded with me. I saw the fear in his eyes. I saw the anger and sadness. I saw his desperation. He pleaded. The owner had sodomized him again. There was blood everywhere, trailing from his ass in a stream of never-ending horror. Why do they call it Man-Love Thursday? It's night. It's Friday before Friday. Remember, remember, they say. Why? Why remember? Why not end it? Why not call a halt and say this is not correct. CoC doesn't want to know. I tried, you know. I did try. I talked to my NCO, but he said it was wine I saw. Down his legs??? I talked to my commanding officer, and he yakked about cultural sensitivity. Do they fuck men in the ass in Afghanistan instead of women? All of them. It's like Sparta, my Classics teacher said boys left their mothers at 7, joined the military to become men. Is it manly to man-love on Thursdays? But he wasn't a man. He was a teen. A boy. A. BOY. A. BLOODY. BOY. AND. MY SERGEATN. DIDN'T. WANT TO. KNOW. MY NCO. DIDN'T. WANT TO. KNOW."

Archie's eyes defocus. His head moves without thought, and he's staring in horror at a brushed-clean brick wall. Where did the brick wall come from? He doesn't remember moving after he began reading Nadine's message. Shock has frozen all perception outside of her words.

The Canadians had whispered to him about Man-Love Thursdays and warned him to stay away from the APN. *I was convoy duty, patrol duty, not training duty, not any other duty. Why did they warn me of something that wouldn't happen? What's Man-Love Thursday? What's Nadine talking about? Who's the boy?*

Archie shudders

Chills race down from his scalp's hair follicles, over the cords in his neck, along the dermis of his skin, shivers into his arms, and shudders his entire self. He doesn't want to read her message, but he must. He doesn't want to think what she meant by "I'm sorry." *And who did she kill? Or did she just shoot him? Maybe she shot him, and he's wounded and in the hospital. "Him" can't be the ex...*

Archie's mind trails into nothingness. Time stops in moments that continue on inexorably. Rough brick scrapes his forehead. He opens his eyes. Grey mortar and clay bricks stare mutely at him. It's a quiet street. He strains to listen. No people are walking towards or away from him. He lays his palms against the bricks and feels their ridges and grooves imprinting themselves on his flesh. A breeze lifts fresh rain scents into his nose. Archie pushes against the wall and turns around. He collapses against it. The wall of mortar-bonded bricks supports him as he scans the street. Cars are parked on the other side, nose to tail, devoid of human life. No car moves.

He's alone.

His heart thuds against his chest wall as he drops his eyes back to his iPhone screen. It's black. It's off. He unlocks it and continues to read Nadine's message, like a moth inexorably drawn to artificial light in the night:

"MY NCO. DIDN'T. WANT TO. KNOW. Neither did the captain. Andrew wasn't my captain then. Andrew was heading up another platoon. My captain transferred me. He said I'd become a liability to my platoon. He said boys like giving their asses at night. It's their custom before Friday. Their day of rest. I couldn't train the APN. I was the best damn trainer. EVER."

Archie nods. Nadine was the best superior he'd ever had. She'd taught him how to patrol, how to eat, and how to relax when they were off duty. She'd organized mock hand-to-hand combat fights regularly. Her only rule was to not actually land blows. She wanted her men ready to fight, not recovering from a fight. That didn't go down well with the men, but rumour had it Nadine's punishments were worse than any drill sergeant's. *We were hyped up, ready to roll, but no one dared cross her*, Archie remembers. But he'd acknowledged her wisdom when, the day after an exhausting no-blows-landed-else-Nadine-would-make-you-pay training, they'd been patrolling a quiet area when suddenly bullets had sprayed them from overhead. One had zinged the very top of one soldier's helmet. They'd all dived for cover. The firefight had lasted hours. They'd begun to ask each other—"How many enemy? Are they rotating in new numbers like some fiendish never-ending escalator?"—when, as suddenly as it had begun, the barrage had stopped. Men had materialized around them, so close that they'd instinctively engaged in hand-to-hand combat, ripping AK-47s out of enemy hands, punching vulnerable temples, slamming bodies into the dusty ground, twisting knives into soft stomachs, as the enemy tore off their helmets, dislocated shoulders, lacerated uniforms, broke noses. Later, Archie had mused that Nadine's rule meant they hadn't started combat with welts and bruise-sore bodies from training. To a man and woman, they'd neutralized all the men. Nadine's training had given them survivability.

Nadine was an excellent trainer.

Is.

She is, Archie says to himself, moving his lips soundlessly. "She is," he repeats out loud, emphasizing the present tense, "She is a good trainer." He unlocks his iPhone and continues to read:

"I was the best damn trainer. EVER."

"Yes, you are," Archie agrees.

"And they moved me. Man-love loves man'love. Men love boys, boys love men, and I can't train. Cause I'm a girl. And men don't love women.

"They moved me. His trail of blood followed me to Andrew's platoon. But she was dead still."

Archie blinks. Who's she?

"He head blinks at me at night, you know. Every fucking night. The therapist says to take my pills, keeps asking me if I take my medications. Like a good girl. Like she was. She doesn't have medications, you know. She didn't have anything to keep her from nightmares, only her Dad. And he did it. He didn't like her. She was in the way of his man-love. But he wanted someone else. Not the man who was a boy, now a man, and trails blood everywhere. He spread it around. I couldn't follow it. It made no sense to me. NOTHING. MAKES. SENSE. LIKE EVER.

"My shrink says to take my medications. I did. He ups the dose, because you can never have too many. I counted my pills. He has no pills either. Blood follows him everywhere like an anal stream that doesn't want to end. It wants to go round and round. Blood doesn't spin. That doesn't make sense, does it? It mixes with her blood and streams onto my pillow every fucking night. My shrink asked me if I'm taking my meds. I'M TAKING MY FUCKING MEDS. I counted them. I have pills to sleep, to wake up, to make me happy. Why aren't I happy? I'm never happy. Her eyes are wide looking up at me, you know, from her throat slit right to her spine."

Stomach acid burns his throat, and Archie mashes his lips together to hold it back, to keep it from streaming out all over the concrete grey. The screen blurs, his knees buckle, his back scours the wall. He catches himself. With a herculean effort, he drives himself upward to a standing position and locks his knees straight. Archie's finger has remained on the screen, and he reluctantly moves the text upwards.

I can't read this!

He lifts his finger off the screen to rub his eyes with all the fingers of his right hand. His hand drops. *I can't read this! Why am I looking at it?* The text clears up, sharpens into individual letters. The screen dims. He puts a finger on the screen. It brightens up again. Archie removes his finger. He cannot read. He reads:

"her throat slit right to her spine. Her vertebrae glisten at me EVERY FUCKING NIGHT. Who did that? Don't ask, my interpreter told me. He looked at her like he sees this all the time. It's man-love. She was in the way. She kept him from the boy because the young man had become jealous and beat the boy senseless then beheaded him too. So this was vengeance. But the young man did what his owner wanted. He'd married his daughter. He told me as I tried to push his bowels back in, his wife was infertile. She couldn't have babies, they tried all the time. Maybe she was too young! He hated it. He wanted his owner. He pleaded with me to give him back to his owner. The blood doesn't stop streaming out of my hands. It drips from my fingers every morning as it pools on my floor. I drag it everywhere in my boots. How can he want to go back?? He beheaded her. SHE WAS 6! What kind of people behead a girl? I saw her playing, you know. I saw her playing the first day I got there. She ran up to me in the compound because I was a girl like her. I gave her candy. We all gave them candy. The boys got first dips. But I looked for the girls so they could share too. She had the widest smile. And her laugh chimed off the mud walls of her compound. I could hear her giggling when I was allowed to enter and talk to the women. Then I didn't see her no more. And her eyes won't stop staring up at me.

"They're green. Dead green. Bright green. I see her laughing under the sun and her staring up at me, and the man-teen crying for his owner because he has a new boy, and his bowels are staring at me, as I'm trying to stop the bleeding, and none of it will stop. The shrink says I have to put him out of his misery. So I did. He wouldn't stop crying, ketp saying he was soryy. Ept saying he didn't want to leave me. He has to leave me. I can't be in my nightmares anymopre. He's gone now. He's at piece. And so amy I awhen si top writing ht-s to I wanted you guys to knw. Cus you're my platoon my back have and you gusy mean weveything to me. You're the sane onews who kno what to do to keep me sane the meds aren't worksing anymore. They never did . I just want people to talk to me to listen to me not to keep interrupting me to tell me to be in the present ain'n tot in the past, notw tevey wagin in the past, stops eltting me I'm ok cause I'm not. And to come back in a week whe at do I dod in the weekg. The therapist wants tme to wotkr again and gets this haunted look in her weyes when i tell her stuff. She nodded liek she totally gets rape, but when she realized not me but him, the boy-teen-man who trails blood out his man-love thursdays and the girl who throat slit in relationsat ofr the boys who died cause he ottok the place of the man, she spat out all thise phrases they learn like robots . She didn't know what to do. She didn't know how to handle it. She got this wooden look of caring. She watned to help but she can't, and the shrink he says ocmeb aci n a week ang do toalk to your peers, but what wyou you guys says if you know the horror?"

Archie's stomach heaves. He clutches his abdomen and averts his head from his iPhone. Vomit stains yellow and green the cleaned grey of the sidewalk. Chunks of turkey and digested lettuce glisten in the stain. Archie closes his eyes and leans back, uncaring about threats nearby. Why hadn't she told Andrew? Andrew could've handled it. Andrew can handle anything. But not this. Archie squeezes his eyes as his imagination chucks full-colour visuals at his inner vision. Blood and remembered screams join the images. He squeezes his eyelids one into the other until stars spurt into the red-blackness of his vision. Therapy doesn't work. Pills don't work. Only the kindness of her platoon. *But we weren't there for her. I saw but didn't want to see. I should've said something.* Archie becomes aware that he's hitting his forehead over and over with his fisted right hand. He halts his fist mid-air and drags in a ragged breath. *I won't say it, I won't say the S-word, but I must honour her. I must honour her by reading her message. They're her last words.* A sob blocks his windpipe, and he struggles against it. At last, he manages to finish reading her message.

"I couldn't tell you the horror. The shrink only listened you know. He let me vent for his 15 before med check. FUCKIN MED CHK! He didn't say anything. Did n'st say one word that mead esense onlyt that I'm not there. But I ma. Every fucking night. Everyt god-damn awulf horrible night. And every fucking day. I had to shoot him. So he could stop crying, and I could stop his bleeding. I had to. I'm sorry. I'm sorry, gyuys I siwh I could bestreonger but ai can't . I want to stlak to somebody who doesn't nod and listen but holds me and lets me cry and soggy his shirt and tells me it's going to be okay then lets me to doi tall over aign the next day. I waltn to alk to somebody who doesn't get that glazed, horror look on their face and spouts automatic phrases that mena nothing but they're taught in school to say to someone when they're hurting because tTHIS IS NOT HURTING. THIS IS PSYCHIC PAIN THAT WON'T STOP. It' wont' stop. Why owont' it stop.

"If onl yp ople whant eod be my friends and weren't afraid o my pain. If only my shrink would let me atlk to him every day, at least he isn't afriad of hearing my nightmares. My truth. Nut he says he has nother patients, he can't see us all every day. He has no time. There aren't anough o fthem to go around. DND won't pay , the fucking government won't pay. No one wants to pay to help us. I wasn't raped. They wnat me to be raped to help me. But it was n't me it was her head and his anus and the boys' intestines falling out. THE OWNER PULLED THEM OUT WITH HIS PENIS. And ican't talke about it because I'm in the present and must remember I'm here in Toronto. An things like that don't happen to normal people who don't wnt ot be my friens because they know the horros I've seen and they don't want to catch what I hv. Youg uys don't wither .I don't blame you. I DON'T BLAME YOU. IT'S NOT YOUR FAULT. I'M AT PEACE NOW."

A scream wrenches out of Archie's throat. "Noooo! No, Nadine, No!" He doesn't care if anyone is around to hear him. Salty tears waterfall over his lashes; his nose clogs up; and he cannot swallow against the lack of air. His eyes itch. He doesn't want to know. He covers his face with his right hand then quickly touches his iPhone so that the screen will not go black.

He wipes his eyes hard as he cries loudly, fresh tears replacing the obliterated ones. He drags his hand down and across his eyes, right to left, left to right, so that he can read her last words. "I used my gun. I know how to gain the system and took it home instead of leaving it in the armoury. I'm calm now, guys. His blood is a pool under his body, but his eyes are closed in peace. Peace at last for the boy, the man, the girl. I'm going to shoot myself in the heart in case they need brains to study. They want to study hockey brains so why not army ones too? Bye guys. You are the best men a gal can have. Don't forget my training."

2059 HOURS

Chapter
22

ARCHIE'S FINGERS WRAP around his iPhone; his eyes fixate on its screen. He squeezes his eyes shut. "Noooooo!" His wail reverberates, stretching and elongating into infinitely silent raging grief. His hand convulses around the plastic edges of the iPhone; the dull pain doesn't register, though it propels him into motion. He swivels on his heel. He walks down the street. At the corner, he steps off the curb and speeds up to beat a car turning left into the street he's just walked out of. His legs lengthen their stride. One, two, one, two, his boots eat up the concrete as he blindly heads towards he doesn't know where. Anywhere but this knowledge he'd blinded himself to.

Ping.

He raises his iPhone automatically and reads the terse message on the lock screen: "Where are you?"

He doesn't know. He has no answer. Archie quickens his steps. He drops his left arm, the one with the hand holding the iPhone, and swings his arms into a counter-metronome to his legs. Archie weaves in and out between slower walkers. He speeds past business men. He hurtles past women running for the bus, their heels clacking on the sidewalk, his boots thumping past them. The sharp bitterness of the women's hot coffees, clutched in their hands, reaches for his nostrils. He bends his arms, curls his fingers, his iPhone disappearing into his left fist, and starts jogging. His strides lengthen. He springs into a run.

He races along the street, not touching anyone as he aims for the gaps between them, their faces and bodies blurring past through his tear-infested eyes. The traffic light before him turns amber, and he speeds up, his lungs gasping to fuel his exertion. Psychic pain drives him across the intersection. Horns blare an angry symphony. Indicator lights blink bullying yellow near his churning legs. Heavily perfumed women rush to use him as a barrier against impatient cars turning right to beat the light change. Archie notices nothing.

He reaches the other side and bolts down the sidewalk.

His iPhone buzzes and pings inside his fist. He doesn't read it. He can't stop to read the messages. He knows they're from Andrew and David. They've read her message, too. Maybe they were there. Didn't David say Andrew was taking her home? Or maybe they had taken her home. He can't remember. He doesn't want to remember. Yet Archie's mind reaches backwards into their conversations. What did they do? Did they leave her there by herself? Did anyone know about the horrors Nadine saw? Why didn't she tell Andrew? They all told him everything.

No, they didn't.

I didn't until today. Not everything, Archie admits, momentarily slowing his gait.

Today, for the first time since he'd come to Canada, he'd told them of the righteous shoot. He'd only hinted at it before now. But Nadine...Nadine had been a member of the platoon long before him. Then he thinks, *she was a senior member. She had authority. Authority can't show weakness, can't disobey orders. She'd been transferred.*

Nadine's shame burns into his shame and flares into a united flame of accusations popping into his mind like evil popcorn—they weren't strong enough, they were weak and self-involved, they'd served their countries, they were heroes, they deserved the balloons and yellow ribbons tied to trees in his old neighbourhood to proclaim their hero status. Heroes can't be weak; their strength can never flag. Civilians expect them to soldier on.

His lips twist into a self-loathing grimace.

"You're weak! Buck up and get on with your life," Stephen's words spear his mind, the memory mushrooming into reality, exploding shame and guilt and pain all over his brain. Nadine must be weak, too, but she wasn't. *Isn't!* No, she can't be dead. But she is. She shot herself. The Sig announces its heft from deep in its conceal carry in his left pocket. The grip is one short move away from his hand.

He skids to a stop at University Avenue. Windows in the tall buildings that line the wide avenue are lit up in squares and rectangles of artificial joy. Cars, trucks, SUVs, vans, and bicycles stream south and north in their divided multi-lanes. Knots of pedestrians wait at each corner for the all-red part of the light cycle to turn green in one direction and red in another. He checks the street signs. He's at Queen Street. The light for Queen turns green, and he runs across. But when his booted right foot slams onto the midway meridian, Archie pauses. To his right, soars the airman and the memorial to the war dead. He looks south. Rectangles of green in the meridian's sunken space puncture the stone paving. Benches facing east and west wait for people needing rest. Planter boxes sprout tall amber grasses, and an obelisk stands waiting for him. He crosses Queen from meridian to meridian, oblivious to honks and cars swerving around him, their brakes juddering, and the gasps of people still crossing University Avenue behind him.

Archie reaches the other side and lopes down the four steps to the sunken space. He follows the paving stone path on its east side and halts in front of the sloping statue to look up at the man gazing north towards the Pink Palace aka the provincial legislature. Andrew had taken him around the St. George campus of the University of Toronto in his first summer in Toronto and included a small history lesson on the adjacent Pink Palace. Archie turns his back on the sight and reads the name under the man sculpted in black stone: Adam Beck.

It means nothing to him.

The sculpted man stands above a stone aqueduct that slopes down towards Archie; a river should be running towards him, but it's dry. Rain drops dot Archie's head. A wind flaps the brim of his Tilley hat. His iPhone pings again, and he uncurls his fingers and reads the message. He holds down the Home button and tells Siri to reply: "I'm at the man in black stone, dried up." Siri sends it, and he powers off his iPhone. He slides it into his pants pocket. He doesn't want it near his heart.

Calmness descends like a muffling blanket over the howling chaos inside him. He looks around at the cars with their headlights haloing in the rain-darkness, their brake lights popping red. Pedestrians clump together, their chatter melting into tires hissing on the wet road. Garlic wafts on the damp air towards him from the high-up high-end restaurants south of him. No one lingers in the place he's in. A cyclist's bell rings, and Archie swerves his eyes south to see cyclists burning rubber west on Richmond across University Avenue. The rain drops increase. They pitter against his skin, and he blinks away the wet. The wind lifts the brim of his hat and strains to rip his hat off. Rain drums faster as the gust disappears. Archie turns his face toward the seamless grey above, and rain dilutes the salt on his face.

Archie walks, head up, eyes forward, along the east side of Adam Beck. He stops as he draws level to the back side of the statue. Dead hydrangeas bob their sepia heads as the wind skitters yellow and red leaves along the stone path. Short trees with their pretty lacework of branches dance in the gusts that blow on and off, their leaves flapping, straining to fly off their wood. The rain picks up as he looks to the west and spots a small alcove inside the back of the statue. It has three steps inside it. Archie surveils the area. No one is paying attention to him.

He deliberately makes his way to the centre back of the statue as he slides his right hand underneath his jacket to reach for the grip of his Sig in its conceal carry case.

The concrete glows whitely in the rain that pummels his hat. Another gust blows up and rips a flurry of leaves from their branch homes; rain plasters them on the ground at his feet. Archie almost skids on their slick surface. He catches his footing and tracks carefully to ensure he doesn't slide again. Small petals dot the grill that runs up to the base of the mottled grey stone base and the three steps that lead up to the three steps inside the alcove. The hydrangeas in their long bed gyrate wildly in the rising storm.

A shout reaches Archie's ears, but he doesn't understand it. His feet propel him up the stone steps as he extracts his Sig. This time, he knows where his broken heart is. It's not in the normal anatomical place, as he'd learnt the first time he was hospitalized. Even though the bullet had grazed him and his shot ignored as a suicide attempt, the surgeon had joked that if he was aiming for his heart, he wouldn't have found it because it was in the wrong place. He used the surgeon's careless joking to mask his interrogation of where it was. This time, he won't fail. He'll stop the pain that clogs his throat and eyes and nose, that crushes his heart with grief that grinds all thinking, all movement, that burns his stomach and tenses his arms into striations of deep aches.

A hand grabs his shoulder as rain lashes his face. The hand whips him around, and he's looking straight into Andrew's eyes. "Archie!" Andrew's mouth mimes against the gale's roaring.

Archie shakes his head and pulls his shoulder out of Andrew's grasp. Archie steps back and hits a massive human wall. He skips up a step to his left and holds his Sig down. He doesn't want to shoot

Andrew or David. It's David behind him, he's sure. He can sense David's familiar energy. He knows how they feel.

"Archie. We couldn't save Nadine. But we can save you."

Archie shakes his head, flinging drops from his hair into the rain, and turns himself to face south, to put both men into his line of sight. David is on his right, Andrew on his left. The pungency of sweat emanates from David. It envelopes Andrew's ubiquitous clean soap smell. Archie steps up a step, backwards. He's at the top of the grey stone steps.

Andrew yells through the rain blowing horizontally and vertically and diagonally against them like a moving waterfall with sources above and beside them. Archie cannot hear Andrew. The headlights of the cars zooming towards them on their east side reflect pinwheels of white light on the storm-blackened road. Wipers furiously whip in semi-circular arcs, back and forth, back and forth, fountaining rain off windshields in futile attempts to clean the glass shields of obscuring rivulets and lakes. But the three cannot see the road, and the drivers cannot see him. He lifts his pistol, which absorbs the rain reflecting light from the windows and streetlights and passing cars. The pistol's matte black disappears it into the statue's shadowy alcove. Sky water streams down Andrew's face. Archie no longer feels Nature's storm. His spirit has left; his mind recedes from human life; his heart strains to keep beating against the force of his father's derision, his twin's contempt, his wife's impatience, his grandfather's suicide. Brains litter the grille in front of him, brains comprising tiny, round, dead petals from the dead dancing flowers hedging the grille on both sides towards the green-covered fountains and the trees that stand guard on either side of this quiet space inside the madding rush of people and their busy lives.

Archie is outside their busy lives. He is outside ordinary life. He is not strong enough, for Nadine wasn't strong enough, nor could Pawpaw face a slow death.

Archie had died that day in New Mexico, although his body remained alive. Years later, his will impelled him to escape north to Toronto, in a last-ditch effort to reclaim his life. But running away doesn't work. Archie steps further back into the alcove. The sharp top edge of the first step knifes the back of his calves. Hard metal digs into his chest, slightly left of his sternum.

A roar of pain, desperation, anger, horror penetrates his hearing: "Archie, no!"

Archie blinks. The roar has a strange sound to it. He blinks against the rain spraying off the brim of his hat and sees David's mouth open, his eyes blinking hard against the blinding water the sky is hurtling down on them and the wind is swirling all around them. David's mouth opens wide. His vocal cords catch breath and bellow out sound. "No! Archie. No! We will help you live. Lean on us, Archie. Lean on us. We will hold you up."

Shock stills Archie's hand, his finger goes rigid against the trigger.

David steps forwards; Andrew doesn't move a millimetre. David lifts his right hand: "Please give me the gun, Archie. Lean on us, Archie." David is yelling, yet Archie can hardly hear him over the maelstrom. Suddenly, the wind drops to nothing. The hydrangeas still themselves. The rain eases, and David's yell is loud in the sudden silence: "Don't shoot, Archie. Lean on me!"

Archie's arm drops, his forefinger falls off the trigger, his hand almost releases his Sig. David reaches for it, his right hand coming up towards where the pistol hangs from Archie's slack fingers. Archie lifts his head sharply and tightens his grip on the weapon in one swift movement. Andrew lifts his palm in a slight gesture, almost hidden from Archie's view. David roots to the spot. He speaks to Archie, looking directly into the shadows of Archie's eye sockets. His hoarse voice bumps over his words like a car on an unused gravel road, but he doesn't waver: "We will carry you for as long as you need us to. We will talk to you every day. We will eat with you. We will feed you. We will walk with you. We will sit in silence with you.

Unlike Job's friends, we are your friends. We are never too busy for you. We didn't see Nadine's pain. She hid it too well from us. And we—" David chokes. He swallows, his Adam's apple bobbing up and down. David surges on. "I lie. It was us. We didn't want to see. She was strong because she felt she had to be. She knew she had to be. She lost her life because she was wrong and right. But you don't have to be silent and strong. We didn't tell her she didn't have to be strong; we accepted what we wanted to see." David gulps. Snot streams out his nose into his mouth as the last of the rain drains off his face. "But we see you, Archie, clearly. Your veneer of health has been ripped away, and we have no excuse not to see your pain. You can be weak with us, and it's okay. Maybe your family, the VA, your old friends, they needed you to be strong, needed you to be normal, couldn't be real with you. But we can. We're not afraid of you or your feelings. Life is about us being there for each other. We will not be so busy that you need to lean on yourself. From this day on, we're going to walk with you in your pain. You can be weak with us, Archie, and it's okay. Why do we exist if not to carry each other when we hurt?"

The trio stand like statues. Archie stares at David pleading with him with unpracticed voice and worried, warm eyes while he leans towards Archie in the darkness between the artificial streetlights. Andrew guards them both.

David says softly, rawly: "Please."

2201 HOURS

*Chapter
23*

Traffic stops. The hum of the city hangs in the air. The rain eases its deluge. And two Canadians, their waterproof jackets and Tilley hats replacing berets keeping their chests and heads dry, their military boots keeping their feet dry, hold their breath, ignoring the dying wind cooling their rain-stained pants.

"Please," David whispers, unable to stop himself. He murmurs, "Battle buddies."

The term catches Archie off guard. The Canadians had avoided using it because of Archie's experiences with so-called battle buddies before and after his secondment with them. Battle buddies in US Military philosophy travel in groups of two or more on and off the battlefield because the whole is greater than the sum of its parts; for Archie, the whole had been the enemy of his individual part. Recognizing that, Andrew had stated, "Battle buddies take care of each other here, Archie. We're your battle buddies, ready to help each other live in civilian life, but we understand your aversion."

Archie mulls the message. David has spoken. Archie strives to absorb that and fails. David sees him as part of a whole that takes care of its parts. Battle buddies isn't abandonment but circling in care. Archie attempts to make sense of the message, but David's voice and the words "battle buddies" only bounce around in his brain without impinging meaning. Archie doesn't want to live, yet his...battle buddy...broke through his own pain and spoke out loud to save him. David...battle buddy? Archie turns the words around and around in his head, hearing them morph from betrayal and mocking to caring. A term he once scorned transforms into David who's there in the night and in the day for him, whose muteness has been his only bandage over his Afghanistan wounds. His friend. Archie rolls that word around his tongue. Yes, his friend. Not just a fellow soldier, a veteran like him, not just a Canadian who had taken him in. But a friend and a battle buddy. His friend has ripped off the bandage of his muteness to save his, Archie's, life. Awe suffuses Archie. His eyes wet, and in the shadowed alcove, he lets go of the certainty that his only solution is to follow Nadine. He casts his eyes left. Andrew's open face returns Archie's gaze, the face of a Canadian army man, solid, committed, dependable. Ethical. Andrew, who'd held him up on Yonge Street, who'd saved him from a homicide beat, remains standing with him, persists in looking for him, willing to stay with him right to the moment of ending his life if by turning away in fear he could lose the last chance to save Archie.

Wonder grips Archie.

Seeing them anew stifles his self-immolation.

Archie cannot let them down.

They are here.

He doesn't know why they, again and again, keep watch for him. Maybe there's hope. Maybe he can hang on to them and so hang on to life. He slides the combat pistol underneath his outer jacket and into his conceal carry. He notices David looking beseechingly at Andrew and Andrew's small shake of the head. Andrew trusts him;

David wants to take away his protection. But Andrew trusts he and David can hold him up, walk with him, and be his real protection.

Archie steps down to join them on the grille. Andrew claps him on the shoulder. Archie nods up at him, unable to speak. Andrew blinks rapidly, his face suspiciously wet. David wipes his face with his seamed palms and short fingers in furious strokes, sniffing loudly, then grabbing Archie and enwrapping him in his muscular arms. David doesn't let go, and suddenly Archie is sobbing on his capacious shoulder while David holds him mutely. David's returning muteness comforts Archie as grief and raw trauma pour out of him. Andrew's unsure hand patting him on the back awkwardly, comforts him. David releases him and holds out his hand to Andrew. Andrew flushes at not being ready, at not seeing the need before it was asked for. He shoves his right hand into his dress uniform pocket and pulls out a small plastic package of tissue. He pulls out three thick tissues and hands them around. The three men wipe their eyes and cheeks, blow their noses, and stuff the tissues into their pants' pockets, making Archie feel for the first time since returning from Afghanistan that he belongs—that he at long last has battle buddies who know his worst nightmares yet accept him, and not only accept him, but will risk having new nightmares to add to their own in order to save his life.

"Right," Andrew booms as he leads them north to Queen Street. "Time for a poppy."

Archie stares at Andrew's back. The poppies are done. Remembrance Day is over. Andrew, sensing hesitation behind him, stops and looks over his shoulder. He catches Archie's puzzled expression and explains with a half-smile, brave in its grief: "There's a tattoo artist I go to. He's available any time I need to remember a new casualty. I'm glad I only have to ask him to add one poppy to my vine." Andrew removes his jackets and hands them to David to hold. He unbuttons his right wristband and neatly rolls up his dress uniform's light green shirt sleeve, and stretches his arm out in the chill night towards Archie for inspection. Archie bends over Andrew's arm as David maintains distance and averts his eyes. A green vine twines up Andrew's forearm towards his shoulder. Poppies dot the vine. A scroll anchors the vine near his wrist. Archie cannot discern the words in the night's contrasting artificial lights. Andrew says to the top of Archie's head: "I am faithful." David says: "John." Archie begins to count the red poppies with their black centres then stops. He doesn't want to know. *Too many casualties for one man*, he thinks. He gulps at the thought that if not for David speaking, Andrew would be off to add two, not just one. *And oh, if only Nadine had spoken of her horrors, there would be none to add today. If only...*

The fine line of the vine is like that thread that parted him from death tonight: so easy to break, yet it held.

Tonight, it held.

Honk!

Archie jumps. Andrew grips his shoulder and holds it for a few seconds until Archie's heart beat slows back to below one hundred. Andrew rolls down his sleeve, buttons the wristband, retrieves his jackets from David, one at a time, pulls them on, and buttons them up, smoothing down their fronts before nodding that he's ready to move out. Archie scans the street in his habitual manner as they march together. The streetlights break through the night air like brilliant fireworks. Passing cars shine like reflecting glass. They splash into puddles, spraying fountains of November rain. Civilians hurry by, huddled into their black puffy jackets, their brown wool coats, their red bomber jackets, their faces a mosaic of joy, of busied worry, of sadness, of nothing, of moving life. The sidewalk supports his striding feet, its cracks and pockmarks vibrant with age. The rain has freshened the atmosphere. Garlic smears the air from a nearby restaurant. Archie's stomach growls contentedly.

The three men turn up Church Street, David and Archie following Andrew to his tattoo parlour. As they reach its entrance with its inserted narrow door, Andrew turns to David: "You'll have time to make it tonight. Take Archie with you." He addresses Archie: "Breakfast tomorrow, Specialist." Archie opens his mouth, then folds his lips together to push them in and out, in and out. Andrew says evenly yet strain making it raw: "I count on you to be there, Specialist. Promise?"

Archie nods.

"I need a verbal answer, Archie. I need to hear you say it." The plea in Andrew's voice startles Archie, and he ejaculates: "Yes, sir. I promise. I'll be there for breakfast."

"So will I," David growls out in his new voice. The two others glance at him, and he glares back, raising his eyebrows, daring them to say anything. Suddenly, they all laugh. Andrew disappears through the door, and Archie and David trot east to Sherbourne, hearing the distant roar of a bus approaching. The bus will take them back south to Queen Street and the streetcar that will carry them to Woodbine Beach on the edge of Lake Ontario.

The Sherbourne bus pulls up, and Archie and David file on. Archie sits in the first single seat; David behind him. A bang catches their attention. The driver has lifted the three-seater on the right side of the bus, opposite to and forward of where they're sitting. The driver returns to his seat and deploys the front-door ramp. They wait.

The nose of an electric blue scooter appears and slams the base of the fare box. The scooter retreats. A moment later, it reappears and once again bangs into the metal base of the fare box and grey driver-protection panel. The scooter retreats out of view. Slowly, the scooter's electric blue nose reappears and touches the driver's panel full on. More of the scooter reveals itself. Pudgy white hands hold the scooter's black handlebars in between bulging white plastic bags hanging off them. The hands turn the handles to the left a little; the scooter reverses out of sight. A moment later, the nose accelerates forward and to the left, missing the driver's panel and bringing the owner of the hands into view. Short washed out blonde-grey hair in a bowl cut. One eye patched, the gauze patch only a bit whiter than her pale skin. Large round glasses half-way down her little nose blend into her round face. The woman backs up her scooter. Archie waits to see what she's wearing. This time, she gets the nose further around the corner. But the left side of the scooter almost jams against the bus's right wheel well. She doesn't turn her head as she reverses again.

Archie decides to count the turning points. How many is it now? Ten? He's not sure, but he begins with ten.

The woman gets her nose further into the aisle and almost makes it, except her back wheels jam up against the wheel well. Eleven. She turns the handlebars and ineptly backs up—twelve—so that when she drives her foot down against the accelerator, she ends up in the same place. Thirteen. The driver says something, his words inaudible to Archie. The woman nods. She pauses. She reverses out of sight. The entire bus watches with Archie to see if she'll reappear.

She does. *That's fourteen*, Archie thinks. This time, her scooter's nose makes it all the way around. Her rear wheels miss the wheel well, and she's in the aisle. *Huh*, Archie thinks, *she made it*, as he goggles at her enormous electric blue and black scooter with its festoon of yellow and white plastic bags and collection of reusable grocery store bags in a red, yellow, green, and blue abstract pattern. She speeds down the aisle past a woman and the man sitting next to her in the three-seater in front of Archie. The man hastens to move his feet out of the way as she skims the front of his legs. The whine of her scooter passes Archie. Her tail lights glow red beside Archie. *Is she going to park in the aisle after the driver flipped up those seats for her?* Archie wonders. A young woman gets on, spots the scooter, does a one-eighty, and disappears off the bus. Archie suppresses an agreeing smile.

The scooter's driver reverses and turns the scooter in a ninety-degree turn so that its rear is against the window opposite Archie.

As she backs up past Archie, her wheels aim for the man's feet in front of him. The man thrusts his legs up and to his left like he's going to fold in on himself.

"You shoulda gotten out of my way faster!" Her voice is like a shockwave in the silent, waiting bus.

"Move ya legs!" She demands of the woman in the middle seat of the three-seater in front of Archie. She waves at the woman to get out of her way. "Move, I tell ya. I'm going there." The woman passenger scuttles over, and the scooter driver turns right and zips down the aisle all the way to the front, her rear facing the back of the bus.

The bus's passengers begin to shuffle. Impatience ripples the air with tension. Archie is in no hurry. He settles comfortably into the red-covered hard seat, wondering if she's going to park at the entrance. But no, she backs up, turns her handlebars to the right, and the scooter's rear hits the seat panel at an angle. She's a bad parallel parker, and Archie eyeballs the size of the scooter versus the space it has to fit into. He wonders if it will. He resumes counting turning points. That one was one.

The woman's returned her scooter to the front, and the man's breath begins to rasp. She backs up, and the man twists his legs to the right in case she backs up all the way past her parking space. She tries again to back into it, but as far as Archie can see, she began in the same place, and so...yes, Archie grins to himself, she's banged into the panel at the same angle again. He itches to guide her, but her set mouth and white doughy hands, which remind him of the movie *Ghostbusters* for some reason, releases him from that idea. Her scooter whines forward at an angle. Archie has forgotten what point he's on. He figures three is a good number. She reverses, and her right side now jams against the wheel well. This is not going well.

Muttering begins at the far back of the bus. The scooter driver couldn't care less. She turns her handlebars to the left and stops and starts forward. Suddenly, she zips backwards and with first a turn one way of the front wheel then the other, she's parked neatly in the space for wheelchairs and scooters.

Archie blinks. He applauds her silently.

The ramp folds back into the floor of the bus. The young woman who'd disappeared hops on and walks quickly towards the back of the bus as the driver closes the door and drives south.

The driver booms: "Welcome aboard the bus to Sugar Beach everybody, the land of pink umbrellas. Sit back and enjoy your ride."

All is back to normal.

"Move your bag."

Archie looks around to see who's said that and to whom.

"Move your bag. That seat is for people not bags."

It slowly dawns on Archie that the scooter driver is looking directly at the woman in the middle seat of the three seater. The scooter driver's white cheeks are pinking. The woman in the three seater doesn't so much as twitch.

"It's the law. You can't put bags on bus seats. It's against the law. You have to obey the law. Move the bag."

Archie angles his head slightly to see better the object of her venom. The seated woman is staring at the scooter driver with confusion writ all over her face.

"Move that bag. It's for people."

"Leave her alone!" The deep male voice from somewhere behind him jolts Archie. His heart hammers.

"I don't have to," the scooter driver yells back. "I have the right to tell her it's the law to move her bag."

"No one wants that seat. When a person gets on, she'll move the bag. Leave her alone!" The baritone voice thunders back.

"How would she like it if I sat there? Maybe I will."

A small voice says, "I'll move the bag. See it's on my lap."

The scooter driver eases her left leg off her seat. Encased in grey sweat pants that stretch around her thigh's girth, her leg slides down until her croc-shod foot is off her scooter's foot well. She reaches down in slow motion and picks up her floppy black bag off her scooter's floor, talking all the while about how if that woman won't move her bag, she's going to sit there because people need the seats not bags. And it's the law.

The man from behind Archie yells: "You can't sit there. You're already taking three seats. You can't take up four seats. Someone else will need to sit there."

"I'm a senior. It's my right to sit where I want," the scooter driver chides. As the bus approaches the next stop, the scooter driver waddles across the aisle and falls into the seat right behind the driver's area with a whump.

The man behind Archie berates her for taking up four seats, whereupon another man from the back of the bus yells: "Shut the fuck up!"

The bus driver shouts down the bus: "Calm down everyone."

Silence.

Archie exhales and lets himself relax back into thoughts of what the women will do.

Thirty seconds pass.

"Get back to your scooter you crazy bitch," the outraged man yells simultaneously with the scooter driver loudly berating the woman next to her, "Keep your bag on your lap and never put it on the seat. But since you did, I'm going to sit where I want to."

Archie's heart slams against his ribs. Heat volcanoes into his throat. His iPhone pings, and he jumps. He snatches his iPhone out of his pocket and reads it. "You got your gun?"

Archie ignores David's jibe. He wants off the bus.

The two men and the scooter driver are now in a free-for-all, each trying to out-yell and out-righteous the other.

Ping.

"C'mon, man, this is the time to use it."

Archie squares his shoulders back like he's trying to fling an insect off his back. He knows David is joking, but he can't laugh as baritone, tenor, and soprano voices fling words around him like bullets in the desert.

"I have the right to sit in this seat. Her bag does not."

"You don't have the right to take up four seats."

"Shut up, all of you!"

"I'm a senior, you can't talk to me like that."

"We have the right to ride in peace!"

Ping.

"Shoot them all!"

Archie launches out of his seat and crashes past the man's legs, stepping on something soft. He brushes past the woman in the middle seat, and her bag flies off her lap behind him, landing with the crinkling sound of bioplastic. He knocks the knees of the scooter driver, who yells at him she's a senior and he should respect her space. A thump behind him heralds her bag landing on the bus aisle floor. He grabs the bus entrance's front right-hand yellow vertical bar as the bus lurches to a stop, and he uses his hand as a fulcrum, letting his momentum swing him around and out through the front door that opens just in time for him to exit, David right behind him.

Archie pounds down the sidewalk for a block, oblivious to the direction he's going in. He halts. David slams into his back, knocking Archie forward. Archie swings around on the ball of his feet and cocks a fist. But David is doubled over, his left hand clutching his stomach.

Archie blanches. "Did I hit you?"

David inhales raggedly and cranes his head up. "N-n-no," David blurts out between fits of laughter. He staggers to his right, his right arm and hand stretching out, until he smacks into the wall. He leans on it, braying with laughter. Archie glares at him, still shaking from the panic that had suddenly filled him while on the bus. David clasps both hands over his stomach and begins howling about the pain. "You're killing me, man. The Sherbourne bus never fails!"

A smile creeps across Archie's face. And then his lips part, and he's grinning. David opens his eyes, spies Archie's face, hiccups as his laughter calms, and grins back.

David releases his stomach, stands up, wraps an arm across Archie's shoulders. "The Sherbourne bus denizens. That's probably the best fun they had all day. You never know what you're going to get on that bus. Did I tell you about the time when...," David regales Archie with his stories while keeping his right arm around Archie's shoulders. David interrupts himself to shoot his left wrist out of his sleeve to check his watch. "We're going to be late. Let's grab a cab," he says.

2300 HOURS

Chapter
24

AT WOODBINE BEACH, David counts out blue five-dollar bills and hands them to the cab driver. "Keep the change." Archie and David climb out of the cab, boots landing in the parking lot's water-filled sunken concrete. The two walk the short distance side by side to the gap in the metal guardrail that separates the parking lot from the grass and sweeping beach beyond. David leads Archie through the gap. They stroll off the worn muddy path on to the dying grass. Together, they cross the paved bike trail and the boardwalk, their boots thundering across the bleached oak boards, notifying the flying gulls that men are here. Archie follows David towards the red snow fences, their vertical wooden slats tied together with metal wire. They lean drunkenly along the northern edge of the beach east to west. One after the other, the two veterans sidle through the space between the first snow fence and the second one. Their boots sink in the soggy sand as they aim for the space between the second and last snow fences and onto the immense sweep of beach beyond. David trudges on, his hands in his pockets, his head bowed to watch his footing. As they draw closer to the water's edge, the sand becomes packed down from the rain and easier to walk on. He raises his head to look at the moonlit surf. Archie follows, sending his eyes along the path of David's trajectory, and spots a small group at the water's edge. The moon shines a long line of light across the pounding waves of Lake Ontario with its unending horizon. Depths underneath the rolling waves hide water's secrets. Like the desert, vast, hidden, open yet vulnerable to wind's will. Archie shivers. I'm more like the lake than the desert. The surf's din grows as they reach the group.

David melds into the group.

Archie stands apart.

Two of the group lean their heads close to David's mouth as he gestures towards Archie; they look over at him and walk with David to where Archie stands. The man, tall and hefty, reaches out a large hand. Archie automatically lifts his right hand to it; the big man's hand engulfs his. The man bellows over the waves cresting high behind him before crashing into the shallow water near them in a billow of white foam. "Welcome to our group. We usually meet at nine, but we're ending the day at 2300 hours as we began it at 1100 hours to remember the dead. And the living," he says meaningfully, his intense gaze holding Archie's eyes. He lets go of Archie's hand, and the woman, short and muscular, reaches out her hand. She smiles widely at him, her cornflower blue eyes shining in the night darkness, as she shakes Archie's chilled hand. "Welcome to our group. Matt and I co-lead this non-denominational service." She leans in and whispers loudly to be heard over the rhythmic din of the wind-driven waves, "Although we use the Anglican Book of Common Prayer. The language is so beautiful, and we are all beautiful in God's eyes. Like this lake whose shores we stand on together. I sometimes wonder what it'd be like to bob on those waves, what lies beneath them, and I'm glad I'm not alone. Who wants to explore them unaided, eh?" she chortles. "I have a couple of diving buddies. They've said oftentimes, 'Let's go out, Cyndy! We'll dive to find what treasures the lake hides, and you can paw through them in the boat where the sunlight is.' They know I'm not fond of the dark." She nudges Archie, squeezing his hand, as she laughs freely. "We could spend a lifetime exploring this mighty lake, eh? It's endless." Her laughter settles into a rueful smile. "I haven't had the courage to say yes to them yet. Unknown treasures and unknown depths scare me. Oh, by the way, I'm Cyndy."

Archie crooks up one corner of his lips in response to her radiant energy, unsure what to say, what to feel. She lets go of his hand, and Archie raises his eyebrows at David as if to ask, "What do I make of this? Should I remain?" A service in church to start the day is one thing. It's ritual; it's familiar. But a service on the beach, its sandy expanse a greyish water-logged reflection of Afghanistan and New Mexico that both holds them up and threatens to pull them into the storm-roughened lake?

A muscular body slams into the back of his calves. "Oomph!" Archie expels air as his arms flail to keep him upright. Steadied, his eyes search for what had assaulted him. An amber-coloured body on four legs, wiggling under the power of its wagging tail, springs after a small white fluffy thing that shoots out from the group to chase a receding wave, its high-pitched barks disappearing under Nature's constant din.

"Hahahaha!"

Archie jumps. He's not used to hearing David laugh loudly. The second time tonight.

David puts his right arm around Archie and his lips near Archie's left ear: "It's okay, man. It's only a dog. Several of the vets have them for emotional support. The service won't bite, either." David grins into Archie's startled eyes. "After this, I'll walk you home. I didn't want to miss this. It's what me and Andrew have always done. Nadine didn't like it, and we weren't sure you'd be into it. But we didn't want to leave you alone. You can watch the surf. It must be alien from where you come from, eh?" David lets go of him as Archie snorts. *Yes*, he thinks, *so much water, enough to drown in after only a few steps into it, is alien to him.*

Cold, wet, refreshing.

Archie longs to feel it rise up his boots to his legs until its coldness ices all emotion. Instead, Archie steps over to the front of the group, near David. The co-leaders begin the service. Archie is surprised to hear them speak from memory, but then, he thinks wryly, they wouldn't be able to see in the dark, and artificial light here would disturb the lake's wild beauty. He surveys the beach of rust-coloured sand and the endless waves that stretch to the horizon.

"Thou will keep him in perfect peace whose mind is stayed on thee." Archie's ears listen as he watches the water, blue-black under the clearing sky and the shining moon, lifting into long waves that race towards him, rising higher and higher until a small line of surf foams at their tops and pulls their crests down to pound into the flattened water below it, throwing whitish bubbly water forwards onto smooth pebbles and sand. The white foam hypnotizes Archie as it ripples towards him: a long line of white spiders, their piston-like legs pulling the flattening wave towards him until the foam vanishes into the sand before the listless dying wave streams back towards the lake, revealing stones glistening red and grey half sunk into the sand, its end consumed by the next crashing wave. Archie feels small against the roaring of this ocean-like lake; he feels insignificant standing underneath the brilliance of the moon, on the beach of sand and stones. Goosebumps erect hair all over his arms in their sleeves. Chills race up and down his back. His leg hairs stand up against his confining army pants.

A Rhodesian Ridgeback suddenly dashes out of the group of men and women facing the two leaders and the lake. He grazes Cyndy's legs, who lets her knees bend, but she doesn't falter in her recitation. A black-and-white mutt with fluffy fur, a short snout, and rapidly blurring paws, runs past Archie's right side, making him jump to the left. The mutt barrels into the Ridgeback and bites at him. The

Ridgeback bounds into the waves, leaving the black-and-white mutt barking her disapproval, all four paws firmly planted on the wet sand, her wide chest thrust forward. Water doesn't stick to the Ridgeback's red wheaten fur as he unfurls his long tongue into the waves appearing and receding over his small paws with their hard claws sinking into the stony sand. Lap, lap, lap. Archie cannot hear the dog slurp with his ears, but his memory plays the sound in his head. The Ridgeback lifts his head, lifts his front paws into the air, rotates on his back ones, and bounces over to the black-and-white dog, who jumps up to nip at his left ear. He shakes her off, his jaw dropping into a wide grin, then trots off down the beach with her in barking pursuit, her fur fluffing in the wind off the lake. A Golden Labrador, a small black and brown dachshund almost invisible in the night, and a white standard poodle glowing in the light reflecting off the waves, leap out of the human group and take chase, their joyous barks disappearing into the wind. The dogs gallop east along the beach. The men and women facing the co-leaders ignore the dogs' happy cacophony. But Archie can't tear his eyes off of the dogs. Only Pawpaw had owned a dog, a collie, for a little while, yet he had no desire to have a dog. Watching the dogs now, their antics fascinating him, Archie's lips part and stretch wide. A desire births deep in his heart to feel that happiness and love for himself. Suddenly, the Ridgeback skids, all four of his paws shoving the sand into a berm; the bigger dogs bowl into him as he digs his front paws into the beach to launch himself towards Lake Ontario. The slender, muscled dog barely touches an encroaching wave before leaping back onto the beach. The dachshund tumbles into the frothy waves. He scampers out and shakes violently, showering drops over the sand. The Ridgeback, Labrador, Poodle, and mutt scram. Feeling better, the dachshund sprints to catch up to the bigger dogs racing each other back to the human group, leaping in and out of the water, snapping their teeth at each other, wagging their tails, stopping and circling each other for a brief wrestling match before resuming their race to the human group, powering past the co-leaders, each dog banging into the humans' longer legs first one way, then the other, before they disappear soundlessly, ears flapping, tongues hanging out, in the opposite direction towards the trees and boulders of Ashbridges Bay Park, leaving behind scents of wet dog. Archie laughs involuntarily, unguardedly.

The co-leaders shout out their words as the dogs play. Over the crashing and pounding, over the white noise of vast Lake Ontario and its windy energy that blows away words yet cannot drown out their intent, they fill their lungs and bellow responsively with each other for the others to hear:

"Let not your heart be troubled...I go to prepare a place for you...I will come again...receive you...that where I am, there ye may be also. John 14..."

Archie shifts his position to see the faces of the small group lit up by the moon above them. Tears spill down some cheeks; others look determined; some look solemn; David looks...

Archie searches for the word for what he sees there. It pops into him as a wave streams up to his boots and splashes over his right foot. "Comforted." *That's the word*, Archie crows to himself in triumph of memory. He sobers, as a wish forms. *I wish I could feel comforted. I wish I could feel happy again.*

David looks over at him and nods with a reassuring smile before restoring his gaze to the co-leaders who are speaking to them all, one with the group, and the group in responsive one with them. Archie doesn't know the words from memory, but that one nod tells him he belongs here. David had meant his words back there on University Avenue.

Archie hangs on to that feeling as he shifts his feet out from the grasping wet hands of Lake Ontario. He steps backwards and huddles closer to the group until he's no longer on the periphery. He may not know these words, but here on this rain-smoothed sand, he stands with David, protected, and knows where he belongs and how he's safe.

2359 HOURS

Chapter 25

Archie stands in the twilight of his bedroom. Alone, he watches the hated clock's numerals shining the time.

11:59.

2359 hours.

One minute to midnight.

Archie crosses his arms, grabs the hem of his T-shirt, and yanks the material straight up and over his head. He drops the shirt to the floor. He stares unseeingly across his bed at the wall with its horizontal bars of artificial light shining in from outside against bars of darkness within. With his left thumb and forefinger, he pulls at the little points on the top and bottom of his belt buckle and releases the fabric belt from the buckle. Archie whisks the fabric from out of the grip of the buckle, and the belt dangles from its confining loops on his pants' waistband. He unbuttons his pants, drags the zip down, and shoves the material down toward the floor. He steps out of his pants. He tugs down the tops of his army-green socks and pushes them off his feet, first the right foot, then the left.

He leaves his socks crumpled on the floor. Only his grey boxer briefs still clothe him. He leans forwards until his hands touch his bed and crawls himself onto it. He curls into the fetal position, rumpling the Arctic sleeping bag and white sheets beneath him.

The seconds tick on.

Slowly, he uncurls himself and pulls the sleeping bag and top white sheet out from under his legs and up and over his body. Archie rolls over onto his back, straightening and angling his legs and arms away from his body. He sucks in air and releases it in one push as he stares up at the ceiling, faintly lit by the white streetlights. He pushes the sheet back down until each damp molecule of air nips his pectorals.

A questioning meow sounds faint through the worn, thick wood of his old door between him and the questioner.

Meow.

Archie holds his breath; he perks his ears. A paw pats his door gently.

He blinks.

Rufus's cat has not once paid him any attention. Questions groove lines across Archie's forehead: *Why is she paying attention to me now? Has she gone blind?*

Archie contemplates this strange turn. But no, she saw him almost 24 hours earlier today, saw him well enough to trot by him without bumping into him as he stood dead centre at the top of the stairs. Worry over what to do contracts his chest. But then he hears the soothing tones of Rufus's wounded voice coming down the hall, an answering happy meow, and a short while later, the pressure change of Rufus closing his door.

Archie remembers the dogs galumphing on the beach, their happiness infecting the group, even himself. He and David had left soon after Cyndy and Matt had lead the final prayers for each of them and those they'd left behind on the battlefields. Exhaustion had descended like wet smog upon him suddenly, and David had said, "let's go," and steered him to the street and a shared cab.

He thinks about how he'd escaped his planned escape from life because two Canadians had searched for him and had not given up on him.

He thinks about the sensations of life fresh and anew to him as he'd walked away with David and Andrew from the statue of his planned death.

Archie's lungs forcefully expel the air he'd trapped in them. The sound alerts Archie to begin his relaxation exercise, starting with his forehead. Archie frowns until he feels the ache down to his skull. He releases his frown. He grimaces until his cheeks tighten up and his eyes squeeze shut. He releases the grimace. He tightens his jaw and compresses his lips until the tension aches his ears. He releases jaw and lips and ears. He flattens his neck into the pillow until the tension pains his ligaments. He releases his neck; relief flows downwards towards the ground. He hunches his shoulders up to his ears, up and up and up. His neck objects. He releases his shoulders back down. He fists his hands, fingertips drilling into palms, and anger floods him. He closes his eyes and focuses on the feel of his muscles and slim bones. His anger abates as he unclenches his hands. He tightens his forearms and upper arms. He cannot tense them apart from each other. They are one in tension. He lets them go.

Archie blinks slowly as blood returns to his arms and head and brings the first stirrings of sleep into him.

Archie closes his eyes and moves his mind to his chest. He feels the strength of his pectorals as he inhales into his upper lungs and stretches his chest up and out as far as it can go. He releases his chest. His heartbeats slow. He contracts his stomach down towards his spine until it feels like there's nothing between his abdominal muscles and his vertebrae. He relishes the strength it takes to suck in his gut and keep it sucked in. Bit by bit, he releases the tension in his straining muscles and moves his focus to his buttocks. Archie squeezes them together until the pain makes him gasp. Faintness assails his head. Archie sinks into it like letting a vortex pull him down into unseen watery depths until an internal alarm far away flashes him louder and louder to release his powerful gluteal muscles. He relaxes deeply into the thin mattress beneath him. Sleep gathers in.

Alone.

No sound surrounds him, not even cars exist.

The silence crushes Archie; he opens his eyes in fright.

The flakes of peeling paint on the yellowed ceiling greet his sight. Archie lets his eyes roam around looking for something: a person, a framed print, a door, a ceiling light unlit. But there is nothing he can see. He reaches out with his ears, but no late-night footsteps echo on concrete, no car races along his street to an unknown destination, no door slams or floorboards creak in this old house in the middle of Canada's biggest city. It's like the entire city has fallen asleep, and he's the only one left awake, left to guard, left to protect all the somnolent civilians out there and in here, in this refuge he'd found while he mothers his courage.

Archie flings his hand out blindly to the nightstand on his left. He touches metal. His hand recoils; his breath breaks molecules apart, scattering them into screaming objection. He sends his eyes this way and that, all relaxation, all sleep gone. With hesitation, Archie stretches his arm towards his nightstand, bit by bit, until his fingertips tap the cold gun. He lets his fingers tip-toe along the handle's warm side and across the gun's gelid chamber. The barrel announces itself to his seeking fingers, and he lets his fingers rest in place for a moment as his mind stops thinking altogether.

Glowing numerals change, and Archie doesn't notice. Absentmindedly, he caresses Pawpaw's faithful companion. The gun's hard metal surfaces comfort the touch of his fingers. He retracts his fingers until they touch wood; he grasps the handle but doesn't let his forefinger thread its way around the trigger. Archie pauses, and his fingers flatten under the gun Pawpaw had given him. The blankness that consumes his thoughts and emotions widens until, suddenly, Andrew's words echo around in the belfry of his mind.

Andrew had caught up to him and David as David and he had exited the cab in front of his rooming house. Exhaustion had leadened all three, but Andrew had tarried long enough to speak words he believed Archie needed to hear.

"Everyone has a purpose, Archie. Your job is to find your purpose. No one can tell you what it is. They can tell you what they see, but your gut knows. Listen to your gut. It will tell you what's right for you. Your purpose is here. Train for it, like we trained for combat. Be ready for your purpose."

Archie's eyes flicker, his mouth convulses, his lips suck in and push out. He moves his head in the murky dark to the left, to the right, to the left, to the right, chanting in his mind: *No, no, no. The waiting is long; it's hard; it's tiring.*

I'm so tired.

Archie's fingers flex and grip the Outdoorsman's handle. His forefinger naturally folds around the trigger. Archie rasps. He sucks air in through his nostrils noisily. The sound bounces off the stained, painted drywall and finds its harmony in an old car with a cracked muffler rumbling on the wet road below his window. Archie forcefully releases the air from his lungs and loosens his grip.

"You have a purpose, Archie. Train for it." Andrew's words replay in his mind.

In all these long years, he thought he'd had one. He thought his purpose was serving his country, fighting for Americans, protecting the land and her people. And then they'd tossed him.

He whips his head to the right and to the left, mouthing, "No, no," his head pushing into the worn-out foam of his pillow, his buttocks pushing down into the flattened foam of his mattress as his back arches. His fingers clutch the gun and pull it towards him. Pawpaw's faithful gun, the one that had shot his grandfather's brains out the back of his skull. The uncaring weapon lies in his hand on the mattress near his hip. November air smothers him. The bodies of soldiers and Taliban and Afghan civilians pummel his remembrance. Expectations from Americans, from his family, that he and the US Army will protect them in a desert land, scour his eyes. Remembered acrid burning of endless pits eats into his nostrils.

Expectations without comfort.

Responsibilities without relief.

Burdensome memories without sustaining support.

From the time he was born, Archie had thought his purpose was his family, being with Pawpaw, defending his country, marrying, starting his own family, and supporting his wife and children and aging parents. And always Pawpaw there with him. And then they'd left him; they'd tossed him and blown his brains into bits.

The dampness of the November night caresses his bare chest, whispering, "let go."

He lies there awhile, hearing the emptiness murmur, waiting for him to move.

He moves...

...his left hand.

He moves...

...his left forefinger into trigger position.

He tightens his forearm...

...and tightens his grip on the gun.

He flexes his elbow...

...and raises his forearm and hand high into the air above his head until he can see his Pawpaw's Outdoorsman's dark body emerge out of the shadows of his room, its edges glistening in the streetlights filtering through the single-paned window and bent blinds. He stares at the gun's blued and wood beauty. The gun becomes lighter than the air feeding his blood oxygen.

He gradually twists his wrist until the firearm is pointing at his forehead.

He bends his elbow more...

...and lowers his forearm until the barrel's point stares straight into his staring eyes. His brain is not worth saving like Nadine's.

He shifts Pawpaw's death instrument slightly to his right until both of his eyes come together to look right up into the empty barrel. He cannot see into the chamber with his eyes yet sees the bullet at its other end, waiting for him to release it.

He cocks his left forefinger steadily...

...and hears the chamber pull itself around and lets slide the bullet into its firing position.

He pulls his left forefinger hard...

Bang!

The wall shakes from the force of a flattened palm.

"Shut up in there! Some of us are trying to sleep!"

Thump! Archie's heart slams against bone. Thump. Thump. Thump.

Bang!

The someone shouts in unison with a palm slamming the other side of the bedroom's far wall. "Shut. The. Fuck. Up!"

Archie hears himself screaming and sits straight up like a zombie reviving.

Archie gasps and squeezes his eyes shut. With his mind, he feels his feet and legs and arms and chest, and then, fearfully, Archie raises shaking hands to his head and touches his hair gingerly, feeling its cut ends spiking against his tough palms.

It exists.

I exist.

I, Archie, am still here.

Breath leaves Archie in a great whoosh.

Where is Pawpaw's gun?

Archie opens his eyes carefully and swivels them around, searching for his Outdoorsman. His pistol, his Sig, announces its hardness beneath him, underneath the mattress. Cautiously, Archie twists his head to the left until his eyes catch sight of his nightstand. There is Pawpaw's death. The gun is lying in its usual place on its accustomed left side.

Grief wrenches Archie. He sobs into his hands, huge lungfuls of tears and cold air, gasping relief in time to the beating outrage from the other side of the wall. Slowly, slowly, Archie quietens.

It was a dream.

A nightmare.

Acting out his deepest desire, the desire he fears and doesn't want, but a desire that doesn't let him go. "My story's not done," Archie whispers to himself. Yet there desire in the shape of a gun lies beside him, a promise of escape to come, the demand to end his story.

Archie lowers himself backwards, stretches his feet towards the bottom of the bed, and stares up at the ceiling, feeling the reassuring outline of his Sig through the beat-up mattress. He remembers his relaxation exercise. He tenses his forehead and releases its ache. He grimaces. Archie tightens his cheeks and releases them. He presses his lips together until bone jabs delicate tissue. Archie releases his lips. His body relaxes. Archie turns onto his left side with a view of the instrument waiting in Canada to kill him.

Not yet.

Tomorrow.

After he fulfills his promise to Andrew.

The clock's numerals brighten. Archie reads them. It's long after midnight.

Today.

Thank you for reading this book.

If you enjoyed it, please encourage your friends, family, associates, neighbours, heck, anyone, to buy a copy or request a copy at their library so that they can enjoy it, too!